BREAKOUT

The SEVENTH WISH

ALL THE ANSWERS

Books by Kate Messner

The Brilliant Fall of Gianna Z.
Sugar and Ice
Eye of the Storm
Wake Up Missing
All the Answers
The Seventh Wish
The Exact Location of Home
Breakout
Chirp

KATE MESSNER

BLOOMSBURY
CHILDREN'S BOOKS
NEW YORK LONDON OXFORD NEW DELHI SYDNEY

BLOOMSBURY CHILDREN'S BOOKS
Bloomsbury Publishing Inc., part of Bloomsbury Publishing Plc
1385 Broadway, New York, NY 10018

BLOOMSBURY, BLOOMSBURY CHILDREN'S BOOKS, and the Diana logo are trademarks of
Bloomsbury Publishing Plc

First published in the United States of America in February 2020 by Bloomsbury Children's Books
Paperback edition published in March 2021

Bloomsbury books may be purchased for business or promotional use. For information on bulk
purchases please contact Macmillan Corporate and Premium Sales Department at
specialmarkets@macmillan.com

ISBN 978-1-5476-0570-5 (paperback)

The Library of Congress has cataloged the hardcover edition as follows:
Names: Messner, Kate, author.
Title: Chirp / by Kate Messner.
Description: New York : Bloomsbury, 2020.
Summary: Moving to Vermont the summer after seventh grade, a young gymnast
hides a secret as she makes new friends and investigates her grandmother's
claim that someone is trying to destroy her cricket farm.
Identifiers: LCCN 2019019160 (print) • LCCN 2019021949 (e-book)
ISBN 978-1-5476-0281-0 (hardcover) • ISBN 978-1-5476-0282-7 (e-book)
Subjects: | CYAC: Coming of age—Fiction. | Farms—Fiction. | Friendship—Fiction. |
Secrets—Fiction. | Sexual abuse—Fiction. | Vermont—Fiction. | Mystery and detective stories.
Classification: LCC PZ7.M5615 Cj 2020 (print) | LCC PZ7.M5615 (e-book) |
DDC [Fic]—dc23
LC record available at https://lccn.loc.gov/2019019160

Book design by Danielle Ceccolini
Typeset by Westchester Publishing Services
Printed and bound in the U.S.A. by Berryville Graphics Inc., Berryville, Virginia
2 4 6 8 10 9 7 5 3 1

All papers used by Bloomsbury Publishing Plc are natural, recyclable products
made from wood grown in well-managed forests. The manufacturing processes
conform to the environmental regulations of the country of origin.

To find out more about our authors and books visit www.bloomsbury.com
and sign up for our newsletters.

For my brilliant warrior-friends,
Anne, Kelly, Laura, Laurel, Linda, Martha,
Olugbemisola, and Tracey

CHAPTER 1

Seagulls and Sabotage

Mia hadn't realized how much she missed the mountains. The countryside rolling past her car window was greener than anything in Boston. She loved the moose-crossing signs and the little villages that felt so sleepy and peaceful. June was in-between season in New England, but in another week, the roads would be humming with campers and fancy cars full of New York City people who stopped to take selfies with cows. For now, Mia loved watching the quiet landscapes drift by. Packing the moving truck the day after school ended had been a hassle, but she really was glad to be moving back to Vermont.

The truth was, Mia wished they'd never moved to Boston in the first place. She wished she could erase the past two years. But leaving was the next best thing, and she'd have the whole summer to settle in. The Fourth of July was less than a week away. Burlington's fireworks were the night before Independence Day and weren't as big as Boston's, but they'd be reflected in Lake Champlain, which made them twice as sparkly. Mia's family could go back to their old tradition—a picnic on the waterfront with sandwiches and Dad's "pyrotechnic brownies" with chocolate frosting and red, white, and blue sprinkles. Best of all, Gram would be there. Summer fireworks hadn't been the same without her catching fireflies in a jar and explaining bioluminescence in the insect world.

"You awake back there, Mia?"

"Mostly." Mia unslouched and straightened her messy brown ponytail. She'd napped her way through half of Massachusetts and most of New Hampshire.

"Good," Dad said, "because . . ." He hesitated a few seconds, then blurted, "I'm-in-Vermont-and-you're-not!" He looked at her in the rearview mirror, cracking up as they zoomed past the Welcome to Vermont sign.

"Good one, Dad." When Mia was little, any time the family took a road trip, she'd beg her parents to stop the car right on the border so the front seat and back seats would be in different states. Mom explained you're not allowed to do that on highways, so instead, the crossing-the-border shout-out had become a Barnes family tradition.

"Never gets old." Mom rolled her eyes, but she laughed, too. Then she passed a pile of day-camp brochures to the back seat. "Hey, you forgot these. I grabbed them in case you need to think more about summer plans."

Mia hadn't forgotten. "No thanks." She tossed the brochures back up front.

Mom held up one with a gymnast on the cover. "There's a new gymnastics camp."

Mia shook her head. "I don't want to do gymnastics."

"That's fine." Dad glanced at her in the rearview mirror. "You can make your own decisions about summer activities."

"Great!" At least somebody was on her side.

"*Provided* those activities involve something other than watching reality TV," Mom said.

"Bummer." Add in some Mountain Dew and Chex Mix, and that had been exactly Mia's plan for the summer. When she got hurt and then had surgery a year ago, she couldn't do anything active for months, so she'd plunked herself down on the couch and watched all six seasons of *Deal with the Sharks* and *American Warrior Challenge*. When her arm finally healed, the doctor wrote a note saying she could go back to the gym, but by then both shows had another season out. So she kept watching.

"You need to choose two activities," Mom said, dropping the brochures in Mia's lap. "One active and one educational. Something for—"

"I know. Something for my body and something for my brain." Mia sighed. "But I think I build muscle just watching those American Warrior ladies. Have you seen them scale the warped wall?" Mia loved how strong they looked. Like nobody would ever dare mess with them. "And *Deal with the Sharks* is totally educational."

It looked like such a fun show to be on if you had the right invention. Once, in third grade, Mia and her friend Alex had made a robot out of old toaster parts from the free pile after the neighborhood garage sale. It didn't do anything, so it wouldn't have been good *Deal with the Sharks* material, but Mia loved thinking up other ideas.

Maybe that's why she opened the brochure for Launch Camp for Young Entrepreneurs. "I might try this one. I could learn stuff to help Gram with her cricket farm."

"Sounds great. But I doubt Gram needs much help now that she's retiring," Mom said.

"I'm not so sure about that," Dad said. "Last time we talked, she didn't sound interested in selling the place anymore."

"You're kidding." Mom left Mia and her brochures alone and turned to Dad. "She had that offer from the man who runs the food-processing plant up the street. It was perfect."

Dad shrugged.

"She needs to think this through," Mom said. "Running

a cricket farm isn't light work. And with her health failing . . ."

Mia opened a flyer and started reading about Knitting Camp. Anything was better than thinking about the idea that Gram wouldn't be around forever. She'd had a mild stroke in January, and even though she'd gotten out of the hospital quickly, the doctors said she had to take it easy for a while. That was the only time Mia had ever seen her grumpy. She'd looked frail, too. That wasn't a word Mia ever would have used to describe her grandmother before, and it had made her so sad.

But for the past few months, Gram had been texting Mia how she'd been going to physical therapy. Now she didn't need a walker or cane anymore, and she'd been doing core exercises to get her balance back. Last week, Gram had texted Mia a picture of herself planking in a new green warm-up suit: *Made it to 45 seconds today!* Gram was still supposed to cut down on stress, though, so she was getting ready to retire. That was the plan anyway. It was part of why Mia's parents had decided to move back to Vermont, to help with the transition.

"Here we are," Dad said when they pulled into the industrial park. Gram's new cricket farm was squashed between the Green Mountain Moose warehouse and an enormous gym.

"Hey, that's one of the camps we were looking at!" Mom reached back and shuffled the brochures until she found that one to wave at Mia.

"I told you, I don't want to do gymnastics." Mia pushed away the brochure.

"But it has Warrior Camp!" Mom opened the flyer to a page with kids climbing a rock wall. "You love that show."

"I like *watching* it." Mia took the brochure and dropped it back in her pile. Why couldn't there be a camp where you had snacks and watched other people climb stuff?

"Ready to check out Gram's new place?" Dad pulled into a parking space next to the Green Mountain Cricket Farm sign, and they headed for the door. Gram had moved everything here right before her stroke. Before that, she'd been raising crickets in her basement. "Gram's excited to give us the grand tour. Bet she's waiting in the lobby with cricket-flour cookies for you, Mia."

Dad was half-right. Gram was in the lobby, but she wasn't waiting with cookies. She was standing on a chair, swinging a broom over her head and swearing up at the rafters, where two seagulls perched on a beam by the window. She looked more like one of the Avengers than an old lady who had a stroke six months ago.

"Mom! What's going on?" Dad rushed over, helped her down, and took the broom.

"These birds pooped all over the place, and who knows

how many crickets they scarfed up before we shooed them out here. And now they won't leave." Gram adjusted the green-framed reading glasses on her head, which had gotten half-lost in her wild gray curls. Then she seemed to remember that her family was visiting. "Sorry. Hi." She gave them all hugs. Mia's was extra long. Then Gram reached for her broom back.

Dad held on to it. "Let's just open the door. I bet the birds will find their way out. You need to relax."

"Relax?" Gram yanked the broom out of his hand. "When someone's trying to ruin my lifework?"

"Aw, Mom . . . those birds aren't out to get you. This is just a little mishap."

"Mishap? No." Gram pointed her broom at the birds. "This is sabotage."

CHAPTER 2

Welcome, Dogs and Sporty Moose

"Wait, what?" Dad looked up at the seagulls.

Mia looked up, too. Then she looked at Gram. "You think somebody did this on purpose?"

"I certainly do. And I know who it was. Chet Potsworth." Gram spit out the name. "He's trying to force me out!"

"Isn't that the guy who offered to buy the farm?" Mom used her extra-calm voice. "I can't imagine he'd do such a thing. Don't you think it's more likely you left a door open?"

"Absolutely not. I'm telling you, Chet Potsworth is behind this. He called yesterday to ask *again* about buying the place. And now we have seagulls. I don't know who he thinks he is, trying to force me out of my own farm."

Mom gave Dad the we-need-to-have-a-conversation-about-this look.

Dad gave her the I-don't-know-what-you-expect-me-to-do-about-it look. Mia could almost see the prickly brain waves bouncing back and forth between them.

Just then, the office door opened, and a fat sausage of an English bulldog puppy came waddle-running out, barking up a storm.

"Syd!" Gram shouted, shaking her head. "She's supposed to be the welcome dog, but we've obviously got some work to do."

"You got a dog!" Mia bent to pet Syd, whose huge puppy head looked as if it might tip the rest of her over.

"You got a *dog*?" Mom said.

Gram ignored her and turned to Mia, who was rubbing Syd's belly. "She'll love you forever now. She only ever barks the first time she meets someone."

"Sorry about that!" A short, muscular bald guy came jogging out of the office. "I didn't know you had people here."

Gram introduced them. "This is Daniel, my new employee."

"New *employee*?" Mom gave Dad the what-the-heck-is-going-on-here look.

Dad pretended not to notice. He shook Daniel's hand. "I'm Steve," he said. "Sylvia's son. This is my daughter, Mia, and my wife, Sharon."

"Nice to meet you." Daniel looked at Mom. "You might not want to stand right there."

"Why?" Mom said.

Right on cue, a seagull pooped in her hair. Her face twisted into the sort of grossed-out, horrified expression you see in modern art paintings when people's faces are melting.

"Hold on and I'll get you some paper towels." Gram headed for her office, and Mia noticed that even though she wasn't using a cane anymore, her walk wasn't quite right. Her right foot was a little droopy or something, so she had to lift that knee up higher when she stepped. "Here you go." Gram came back, handed Mom the paper towels, and pointed to the corner. "Bathroom's over there."

As Mom left to clean up, Daniel turned to Gram. "Sorry I can't stay longer. I have to leave for practice at ten."

"Practice for what?" Dad asked.

"Lake Monsters." Daniel swung an imaginary baseball bat. "I used to play growing up in the Dominican Republic. When I moved here for grad school and had Sylvia for class, she suggested I try out for the team."

"That's so cool!" Mia had forgotten Burlington had a minor league team.

"Shoot, that reminds me," Daniel said. "We have a

game a week from Saturday, so I can't staff our farmers market booth the whole time. I can ask James to cover for me if you want."

"Absolutely not," Gram said. "He'll want to be at the ballpark, cheering on his beloved husband. Maybe Mia can help."

"I'm . . . busy then, I think." Mia couldn't imagine standing at a booth at City Hall Park, selling cricket protein powder to strangers. But she felt bad letting Gram down. "I can help now, though, if you want."

"Actually, we need to get going," Mom said. She'd just come out of the bathroom, rubbing her damp hair with a paper towel.

Dad nodded. "Do you want to come with us and see the new house?"

"I can't," Gram said. "I have a meeting with a contractor for the new air filtration system."

"New air filtration system?" Mom pressed her lips together. "Mia, would you give us a few minutes? You can check out that gym with the fun camp."

"Sure." Mia hugged Gram and went outside. But the last thing she wanted to think about was gymnastics, so she turned away from the gym and went to see what Green Mountain Moose was all about.

The front windows showed off a big office with a wall full of stuffed toy moose, all wearing clothes and carrying props. There was a white-coated doctor moose with a stethoscope around its neck, a businessperson moose with a briefcase, and a construction worker moose with antlers sticking out from under its hard hat. Another shelf was full of moose athletes—a soccer moose and a football moose and a figure skater with its hooves stuffed into skates.

"Do you play a sport?" somebody said, and Mia jumped about a mile. When she landed, a short, sturdy man with spiky gray hair was backing away from her with his hands up, laughing. "Sorry! Didn't mean to scare you. I'm Bob Jacobson. I run this zany moose company. Is Sylvia your grandmother?"

Mia nodded.

"Thought so!" he said. "You're Mia, right?"

She nodded again. How did the Moose Man know her name?

"Your grandma's talked a lot about you. Don't you love our sporty moose?" He gestured to the shelf of athletes with antlers. "Let me guess . . ." He looked Mia up and down in a way that made her want to put on a big parka. "I bet you're a runner!"

"No, I'm a—" Mia almost said "gymnast" but remembered she wasn't anymore. "I don't play a sport." She was grateful when her parents came out of the cricket farm.

But then she realized they were arguing. With more than just their eyes.

"This was *not* the plan," Mom said. She'd never been a fan of the cricket farm in the first place because she said it was another one of Gram's far-out ideas. There was nothing far-out about Mom. She liked sensible shoes, a sensible haircut, and sensible jobs. Cricket farming wasn't in that category. "We moved back to help your mother transition—not to help her take care of a million crickets."

"She's not asking for help."

"She needs to cut down on stress."

"She needs time," Dad said. "She'll see." He looked around. "Mia, let's head out!"

"Coming!" Mia turned back to the Moose Man, said "Nice to meet you," and hurried to the car. She hoped her parents would stop talking when she got in, but they didn't.

"I know you still think your mother is some kind of superhero, but she's too old for this. Did you hear what she said? She thinks someone's *sabotaging* her farm."

"I know." Dad pulled out of the driveway. "I mean, it's possible, but . . ."

"She's not thinking clearly," Mom said. "You know her stroke affected the left side of her brain, and that can impact logic and reasoning. It's time for her to step back from all this."

Mia looked down at the pile of brochures on the seat next to her. She couldn't listen to her mom talk about Gram like that anymore, so she changed the subject to the one thing she thought might get her attention. "I'll do that Warrior Camp!"

It worked. Mom turned around. "That's great! I'll get you signed up for that and Launch Camp tonight. I bet you'll really enjoy it!"

Mia nodded, even though she knew she'd hate it. But at least the Warrior Camp was close to Gram's cricket farm. Mia would be able to spend some time with her and make sure Mom was wrong. Gram might be walking a little funny, but her thinking was just fine. Mia would make sure. And she'd be able to help out with chores so Gram could keep doing what she loved. Because if she couldn't . . . well, Mia didn't even want to think about that.

Boxes from the Attic

Mia and her parents picked up Vietnamese takeout for dinner. The movers had already delivered their furniture and boxes, so after they ate, Mia went to her new room to unpack. It was bigger than her room in Boston, which was good because Gram had made her parents take back all the stuff they'd stored in her attic when they moved away.

The two old boxes from Gram's house that belonged to Mia were by her bed now, labeled Mia's Room in her little-kid, Magic Marker handwriting. The rest of her boxes said the same thing but typed on the Boston moving company's labels. Mia lifted a flap to look into one of the older boxes. It was full of third-grade homework papers and dried-up cicada shells from the trees behind Gram's house and gymnastics trophies from her old team in Vermont.

It was funny. Mom had said moving back would be like coming home. But that wasn't true. Practically Mia's whole life here had been about gymnastics, and that was gone now. Her old best friend Lily had moved to Seattle last year, and her friend Alex, who lived next to Gram, was off at camp until fall.

Mia rummaged through the box until she found some pictures. There was one of Mia and Alex with their toaster robot, one from Lily's ninth birthday party, and one of Mia jumping off the red rocks into Lake Champlain.

Mia pulled out that picture and tried to remember what it felt like to be standing on the rocks in her rainbow swimsuit. That girl looked so different from the way Mia felt now. Those rocks were pretty high. You had to run a few steps so you could leap way out into the deep water, and some people stood at the top forever trying to get up their nerve. Not Mia, though. She'd jumped in right away the first time her parents took her there, on the hottest day of the summer after third grade. The water had been so clear, so cold it took your breath away. The rocks had been so red and the sky so perfectly blue, and when Mia leaped off those rocks, she'd felt like she could fly. Like she could do anything. She couldn't imagine feeling that way now.

Mia dropped the photo in the box and shoved the whole thing deep into the back of her closet. She didn't have time to be poking through old floor routine programs and Barbie dolls. She had to deal with the stuff she needed now.

Mia put on some music, unfolded the sheets her mom had left on the dresser, and made her bed. She found Neptune, the stuffed stingray she'd gotten from the New England Aquarium, and put him by her pillow. Then she loaded her shorts and T-shirts into her dresser, hung her two dresses in the closet, and shoved the bin with school clothes and sweaters off to the side. She'd deal with those in September.

The next box Mia unpacked was full of gymnastics posters, but Mia didn't want those in her new room. Waking up to a poster of Simone Biles on the balance beam felt different when you were never going to set foot on one again yourself.

Mia tucked the posters back in the box. The movers had already put her mirror up on the wall over her dresser, so she found some photos to go around it—one of her family watching the Boston Marathon and one of her cousins together at a cookout last year. Her littlest cousin, Fiona, was wearing Mia's gymnastics T-shirt over her swimsuit. It was way too big, but Fiona loved Mia's hand-me-downs whether they fit or not. She always wanted to be just like Mia.

Mia put up a bunch of photos she'd taken with her

photography club at school. They were mostly fall leaves around Boston Common, but one was a picture of Mia from when her friend Eunice had grabbed the camera. It was before her accident, but the Mia next to the maple tree already had a tense, squinty look on her face, like she knew something bad was coming.

The next morning after church, Mom, Dad, and Mia headed back to the cricket farm so Gram could give them a tour now that the seagulls were gone. As soon as they opened the door, Syd waddle-ran over. As promised, she didn't bark this time. She wagged her tail, flopped down, and rolled over for a belly rub.

Gram was waiting in the lobby to greet them, too. But she still didn't have cookies. Just a big jar of bugs. "Have some roasted crickets!" She gave the jar a shake. "They're good for you!"

"I'd rather have coffee," Dad said, "and a hug from my mom." He leaned in for one.

"Food is love," Gram said.

"Yes, but that's not food. Unless you're a pet lizard." Mom hugged Gram, too, careful to avoid the jar. Gram had been raising crickets for almost three years now, and Mom still refused to even try one.

"Mom's feeling a little 'bugged' by this situation," Dad said, but no one laughed at his joke. "Nothing but crickets, huh?" He paused. "Get it? Crickets?" Dad cracked himself up.

Mia reached for Gram's jar. "Crispy Cajun?"

"New recipe."

Mia shook out a handful and popped them in her mouth. She knew that would make Gram happier than any hug. Gram had been the first female entomology professor at the University of Vermont. She'd given Mia a butterfly net and "critter condo" for her seventh birthday, and they'd spent hours stalking grasshoppers in the garden. When Gram first got interested in entomophagy—eating insects as food—Mia had been right beside her, testing recipes.

"These are pretty good!" Mia said. "But I still like the garlic and sea salt ones best."

Gram nodded. "We'll be able to offer more flavors now that the expansion is underway."

"Expansion?" Mom sounded like she had a cricket stuck in her throat. "Sylvia, I wish you'd talked with us about all this. Last I knew, you were getting ready to sell."

"I changed my mind," Gram said. "Insects are the future of food. I want to be part of that."

Mom looked at Dad. Then she looked back at Gram.

"But what about your stroke? You were going to take it easier now that—"

"Pfft." Gram lifted her arm and made a muscle. "There's nothing stronger than a woman who's rebuilt herself. I've been doing my PT, and I'm ready for anything. Now come see the new place."

Gram opened the door to the cricket room, and Mia went in first. "Whoa . . . this is impressive." It was the size of Mia's school gym, with four long rows of big rectangular boxes, all filled with chirping crickets.

"Daniel's bringing in fresh feed." Gram nodded toward the back door, where Daniel was lugging in a big sack. "This'll all be easier when I can hire more people."

Mom took a deep breath. "Sylvia, we're concerned. A few weeks ago, you were all set to sell. Isn't your buyer still interested?"

"Chet Potsworth?" Gram looked at Mom as if she'd just suggested selling her cricket farm to a skunk. "That man needs to learn how to take no for an answer. I'm sure those seagulls are his doing."

Mom pressed her lips together. She gave Dad the this-is-what-I'm-talking-about look. Dad just looked like he wanted to go to brunch. Also like he wanted to get Mom out of there before Gram said anything else. He glanced at his watch. "Wow, I didn't realize what a late start we got today. We've got unpacking to do, so—"

"Can I stay and help Gram?" Mia asked. "I got my room set up last night."

"I'd love that," Gram said.

Mia looked at Mom, who nodded. "Sure, we can pick you up in a few hours."

As soon as Mom and Dad left, Gram's phone rang. "I should take this." She called across the warehouse. "Daniel! Mia's going to help. Can you show her what needs to be done?"

"Sure! We'll have you trained as a cricket caretaker in no time," he said as Gram left for her office. "Let me introduce you to water dish duty."

At first, Mia stayed back. She always felt uncomfortable around new people now, even friendly ones. Especially friendly ones sometimes. But Daniel gave her space and showed her how to rinse out the crickets' dishes. Something about him put her at ease.

"If there are any crickets in the way," he said, "just blow on them, and they'll move."

Mia went to a box and found the water dish full of crickets. She blew a light stream of air at them, as if they were birthday candles, and sure enough, they vanished into their little cardboard cricket cubbies. Except for a few lying still in the water.

"I think I have some dead ones in here," Mia said.

"How many?"

"Four."

"That's fine," Daniel said.

Not if you're those four crickets, Mia thought. "Did they drown?"

There wasn't much water in the dish, but Daniel nodded. "Crickets may be a superfood, but as a species, they're dumber than a bag of banana slugs. They're totally capable of climbing out of the water; they just don't know enough to save themselves. We lose some every day."

Mia looked down at the poor drowned crickets. They should have just jumped out of that water. Stupid bugs.

But she felt bad for them anyway as she brushed them into the garbage. When you were the person who showed up to rinse out the water dish, it was so obvious what should have happened. But it was harder to see the solution when you were the one drowning.

Mia rinsed out four more water dishes. The last one had a dozen dead crickets, and Daniel was concerned about that.

"Can't you give them less water?" Mia asked.

"Not really. It'd evaporate too fast, and we don't have staff to be adding water all day."

"What if you did it automatically? Like those sprinklers in the produce section at the grocery store." Mia had loved those when she was little. She'd wait and wait so she could stick her hand in above the broccoli and feel the cool mist.

"That's actually a great idea," Daniel said. "I'll ask Sylvia about it if the next round of funding goes well."

"Gram's trying to raise more money?" That was news to Mia, and she was glad Mom wasn't around to hear it. "Is that because she wants to expand again?"

"She doesn't just *want* to expand," Daniel said. "She *needs* to. In order to be profitable. We've had so many issues—with temperature and humidity and now seagulls. We need to start producing more crickets. We can do that if we expand, but we'd need another five hundred thousand dollars by the end of the year."

"Whoa," Mia said. That was more than most people even asked for on *Deal with the Sharks*. "Who's going to give her that kind of money?"

"Angel investors. Hopefully."

"Angel investors?" Mia tipped her head, imagining the chubby angel from the stained glass window at church, showing up with a big check.

"People who invest in a small business, with the understanding that it may or may not end up succeeding," Daniel said. "They're hoping it'll end up being the next Google or Apple."

Mia looked around at all the cricket condos. As much

as she loved Gram, it was hard for her to imagine some serious businessperson investing half a million dollars in a room full of bugs. "What if she can't raise the money?"

"Then I'm going to need a new job." Daniel sighed. "We're out of options here. It's either come up with new investors or shut down the farm."

CHAPTER 4

KicksFinder, the Bao Bus, and a Robot without a Job

There should have been pancakes and bacon on the first Monday of summer vacation. Mia should have slept in until at least ten and maybe later now that she was almost a teenager. She should have had the whole lazy day to herself to watch TV and find out if Elizabeth "Cat Lady" Marino would finally make it through the ultimate extreme warrior course.

Instead, she was up at seven to say goodbye to Dad, who was driving to Boston to meet with real estate agents about their old house. By eight, she was walking into the middle school for Launch Camp. A lady with short black braids and a neon-green T-shirt was standing outside, bouncing. Literally bouncing. Her voice was even louder than her shirt. "Welcome to Launch Camp!" She looked down at a clipboard. "You must be . . . Mia!"

Mia nodded.

"I'm Zoya. Go ahead to the maker space," she said, pointing down the hall. "That's where we'll have orientation. I need to make a few copies and I'll be right down."

Mia headed for the maker space. Her school in Boston had one of those, too, but it was always full of eighth grade boys who didn't look excited to share it, so Mia never went in there.

But at this school, the maker space felt different. There were two big tables covered in scratches and paint drips and a row of computers along one wall. Another wall had shelves full of books, paper, colored pencils, duct tape, Legos, buttons and switches and other electronic-looking parts, hot glue guns, and rolls of string and wire and ribbon.

On the far side of the room was a glassed-in workshop with a long bench and tools hanging on the walls. A boy and a girl were leaning over the counter, sorting bits of metal into containers. The girl had a freckly face and red hair in two long braids. If they'd been sticking out straight, she'd look like that Pippi Longstocking girl from the stories Mom used to read Mia. The boy next to the Pippi girl had shaggy blond hair, and his feet were resting on a skateboard under the table.

At the other end of the glassed-in area, a girl with long black hair and sparkly silver nail polish was messing with wires on some kind of robotic arm. It reminded Mia of the robot she and Alex had made, except this one looked like it might actually do something.

Other kids sat at tables, grouped in pairs, taking notes or huddled around laptop computers. One of the computer boys looked up at Mia. He had sandy-brown hair, bright blue eyes, and the kind of dimples that Mia's friend Eunice loved. "Are you hardware or software?" he asked, drumming his fingers on the table.

Mia wasn't sure what he meant, but she was pretty sure she knew the answer. "Neither." He looked so unhappy that she added, "I mean, I'm okay with computers, but I don't write code or anything, if that's what you're asking."

"That's okay," the boy said. "We can use you for our social media campaign."

"*Use* her?" The girl next to him gave him a swat on the arm and shook her head. "She might have her own plans, you know." She adjusted the zebra-striped headband that was trying to hold her blond curls out of her face and turned to Mia. "Sorry. Eli's obsessed with KicksFinder and tries to enlist everyone to work with us. I'm Clover, by the way. That's Nick." She nodded to a boy with spiky brown hair next to Eli. He waved without looking up.

"I'm Mia. And I really have no clue what I'm doing yet. But what's KicksFinder?"

"It's an app we wrote," Clover said. "It's for—"

"It's going to be huge," Eli said. "And when we roll it out—"

"Dude." Clover held up her hand. "You interrupted. Let me finish." She turned back to Mia. "It's for soccer players. When you share your location on the app, it pulls up a map and shows you all the pickup games at nearby parks." She held up her phone to show Mia. Their location was flashing on a map, but no games showed up nearby. Probably because everyone was home asleep or eating pancakes and bacon.

"That's cool," Mia said. "But . . . how do you already have so much work done? Isn't today the first day of camp?"

"Yes, but most of us were in the school makers club with Zoya last year," Clover said. "She said we could work on the same projects if we're using them for the competition next month."

"Competition?" Mia should have read that brochure more carefully.

"Vermont Launch Junior. Five weeks from Saturday!" As soon as Eli said that, his eyes got wide. "Shoot. We have so much to do." He turned back to his computer.

Clover laughed. "The competition is optional. It's the

junior version of a program for adults who want to start small businesses. They present their projects and compete for funding from investors. If you win the junior version, you get a fifty-dollar check, a trophy, and the chance to work with a mentor. Also, the project gets written up in the newspaper, so that's cool."

It sounded a lot like *Deal with the Sharks*. Mia looked around. "Is everybody doing the competition?" She didn't want to be the only one who wasn't.

"Well . . ." Clover pointed to the robot girl. "Probably not Anna. She's building a robot, but it doesn't really do anything practical. You need a business plan for the competition, and she doesn't have one. She just likes building robots."

"Who's Anna working with?" Maybe Mia wouldn't be the only one without a team.

"Nobody." Clover lowered her voice. "She was working with us on KicksFinder, but Eli likes her. He was always looking at her and asking her to go for ice cream after camp, and even after Zoya told him to quit it, Anna was still uncomfortable, so she decided to go off and do her own thing. She likes robots better than apps anyway."

"Oh." Mia watched Anna fiddling with her robot wires and understood why that was better than writing code next to someone who kept staring at you all the time. "What about everybody else?"

Clover pointed to the Pippi girl and the skateboard boy. "Julia and Dylan make jewelry out of recycled metal, and they're doing the competition. So are Quan and Bella." Clover nodded toward two kids at another table. The boy had short, spiky black hair and glasses, and the girl looked like she might be his sister. She had the same dark hair, but hers was wet and dripping onto the shoulders of her Champlain Valley Swim Team T-shirt. "They're starting a Bao Bus to sell dumplings from their family's restaurant. It's actually going to be more like a cart, but Bao Bus sounds cooler." Clover pointed to the last kid, a tall, skinny, curly-haired boy in a baseball uniform. He was bouncing his knee and drawing something with colored pencils. "And that's Aidan."

"What's he doing?" Mia asked. "Writing an app to find baseball games?"

"Nope. He's designing his logo for Cookies for a Cause. Aidan bakes great chocolate chip cookies, so he's launching a business to supply baked goods for fund-raisers. He's just in the uniform because he has a Little League game later."

"Wow. That's . . . great." The projects were better than Mia expected, which was cool but also kind of terrifying. She hadn't been here when everybody chose their projects. Where was she even supposed to start?

Zoya bounced into the room with her copies then. "Gather around, and let's get going!" When everyone was seated, she ran through the itinerary for camp, including some special days when they'd have guest speakers or field trips. She showed pictures of past camps, too, and the kids' projects. All the kids in the pictures seemed to be having a pretty great time. Mia was actually starting to look forward to this.

"So, Mia . . . ," Eli said after Zoya's introduction. "Do you want to work on KicksFinder with Nick and Clover and me?"

"Thanks," Mia said, "but I don't think I'd be very help-ful. Also . . . I might want to work on something else."

During the slideshow, Mia had found herself thinking about Gram's cricket farm. Maybe helping Gram could be her summer project.

"Is it okay if we come up with new ideas for a business that already exists?" she asked Zoya. "Not for the compe-tition. Just for fun."

"A business you're connected to somehow?" Zoya asked. "Like through family or friends?"

Mia nodded.

"That's a great idea," Zoya said. "Start-ups need to begin small, but it's important to innovate and grow. You're thinking about ideas for that?"

Mia nodded again.

"Then go for it!" Zoya said, and moved on to talk about jewelry pricing with Dylan and Julia.

Mia thought about what Daniel had said about the farm needing to grow to survive. About the issues they'd had with humidity and temperature and the poor crickets drowning because they were too dumb to climb out of the water. About how Gram was always saying people would love crickets if they could learn to see them as food.

Maybe Mia didn't have a robot in progress, or a completely coded app, or two boxes of recycled jewelry ready to go. But she had some ideas. And that was a start.

CHAPTER 5

Business Plans and Beetles

On Tuesday, Zoya bounced into Launch Camp and started the day with a presentation on business plans. "You need a game plan," she said. "Something to share with potential investors. But a business plan is also important for the entrepreneur. When my parents emigrated from Iran in the seventies, they opened a bakery. Their business plan allowed them to start off small and grow. Now they employ forty people in Los Angeles."

"How come you work here and not there?" Eli called out, tipping back in his chair.

"Because I'm at UVM, getting my graduate degree in sustainable innovation—studying how businesses can grow in ways that don't harm the environment. Now put your chair down so you don't crack your head open, and let's get going on your plans." She passed out copies of a template. "I know most of you are already in the thick of it, making products and debugging software, but take time today to jot down ideas."

Eli sighed at that, but Mia wasn't in the thick of anything, and she was grateful for the direction. She started filling in the template.

IDEA: Cricket farm

After that, she felt a little stuck.

"Any questions?" Zoya asked, leaning over the table.

"I'm not sure how to do this because it's not a new business. My grandma's already running it, so she must have done something like this to get her first investors."

"Sure. But you should still fill this out to get thinking. You can compare it to hers later on." Zoya tapped the word "idea." "What you want to think about is *why* it's a good idea. I'm assuming one of your goals is to expand the market?"

That sounded good, so Mia nodded.

"And these are crickets for pet food?"

"Nope. People food," Mia said. "They're super healthy if you can get past the fact that you're eating bugs."

"Ahh . . . ," Zoya said. "So can you make a case for

eating crickets so a reasonable person would want to try them?"

"I think so," Mia said. "Okay if I use a computer to do some research?"

"Of course." Zoya went to see how Quan and Bella were doing with their not-quite-a-bus Bao Bus while Mia moved to a computer. She scrolled through a list of articles about crickets as food, and most of the information was familiar. Gram always talked about how a serving of crickets has more protein than a serving of beef or chicken and how they're better for the environment, too. Mia thought it was cool that raising crickets used up to twelve times less feed and two thousand times less water than raising beef.

Most people didn't know any of that. Mia wondered if Gram could have an open house like they did at the maple farms when they demonstrated how syrup was made. She added that to her business plan.

Mia read through some more articles. She'd just clicked on one about a major league ballpark serving fried grass-hoppers at its concession stands when Zoya called, "Ten minutes left!"

Mia couldn't believe two hours had passed. She added *Check on ballpark concessions for Lake Monsters* to her plan and saved that page for later.

It was only two blocks from the school to Gram's house, so Mia walked over after camp. The warm, sweet scent of bananas and cinnamon swallowed her up as soon as she opened the door. Gram stood at the counter, stirring up a batch of banana bread batter, wearing her Eat What Bugs You apron. It had a little cartoon cricket with a chef's hat that said Hop Chef.

"Hi, Gram! Need some help?"

"You're just in time. Want to grease another loaf pan for me?"

Mia put down her backpack, washed her hands, and coated the pan with cooking spray.

"How was your camp?" Gram asked.

"Interesting." Mia held out the loaf pan so Gram could pour in the batter. "It got me thinking about ideas for the cricket farm."

"You always were my best helper," Gram said. Mia didn't mention that she was making a whole new business plan. Gram was already stressed out about people telling her what to do.

But not telling Gram made Mia feel funny, too. Before Gram's stroke and Mia's accident, Mia had always told Gram everything. Even after they moved to Boston, Mia would text to share little things that happened at school. Lately, though, the things Mia didn't talk about felt like a big tower of boxes stacked up between them. Leaving out that part of Launch Camp felt like throwing another carton on the pile. Pretty soon, she wouldn't be able to see

Gram anymore. But there were some things you couldn't say out loud.

"Is this a new recipe?" Mia asked so she'd stop thinking about the boxes.

Gram nodded. "Trying to see if I can get the protein content up a little more." She went to the sink to rinse out her mixing bowl just as the oven timer went off.

"Want me to see if it's done?" Mia asked, reaching for an oven mitt.

"Remember how to check?"

Mia laughed. "Gram, just because we haven't baked together in a while doesn't mean I forgot everything!" She took a toothpick from the cupboard, opened the oven, and poked it into the bread, just like Gram had taught her when she was little. It came out clean, with just a few crumbs sticking to it, so Mia set the loaf on the counter to cool.

It smelled amazing, and Mia was grateful when Gram asked her to do a taste test. "Let me know what you think," Gram said. "I might need to adjust the recipe before we share it."

Mia cut a slice of bread and blew on it to cool it. She took a bite and chewed thoughtfully. "It's good," she said, "but maybe a tiny bit gritty?"

"Guess I was a little too enthusiastic. I'll have to tweak the flour-to-cricket-powder ratio." Gram looked at Mia and sighed. "Sorry you had to be my guinea pig. Other people's grandkids get nice reliable chocolate chip cookies, and you're stuck testing cricket recipes."

"I like being your guinea pig," Mia said. "And this is still really good." She took another piece so Gram wouldn't feel bad. It wasn't Gram's fault that she loved crickets more than everybody else did.

Mia put the last batch of bread into the oven and dried dishes while Gram washed and hummed along with the radio. Even with the boxes piled between them, and even on a day she had to taste test gritty banana bread, with Gram was still Mia's favorite place to be.

When all the bread was done, Mia and Gram had lunch and drove out to the cricket farm. On the way, they passed the Chocolate Shoppe, which had an Open House sign out front.

Mia pointed it out to Gram. "Have you ever thought about doing an open house like that for the cricket farm? We were brainstorming ideas at camp, and that was one of the things I came up with."

Gram raised her eyebrows as she flicked on her turn signal. "That's an interesting thought. We can't have people traipsing through the warehouse, but I could set up a display in the lobby with bins of crickets at different stages in their development."

"You could give out samples, too. And have posters about how healthy and sustainable crickets are."

"I like that idea!" Gram smiled at Mia as they pulled into the parking lot. It made Mia feel like the stack of secret boxes between them got a little smaller.

Gram looked at the calendar on her phone. "What if we plan this open house for . . . August ninth? Sunday afternoon's good, right? That'll give us five weeks to get the word out. And the summer tourists will still be around."

"I can help with decorations and everything," Mia said.

"Perfect!"

Mia followed Gram inside. Gram still had that kind of funny walk, but she was moving along. And she didn't seem like she was having any trouble thinking, like Mom had suggested. Gram was fine. She could make her own decisions about whether to sell the farm or not.

Mia was about to ask Gram if she could see the original business plan when Syd came wobble-racing out, looking for love. Mia was tied up with belly rubbing for a good five minutes, and by then, Gram was on her phone.

"Hey there! Here to help?" Daniel asked, holding open the door to the cricket room.

"Sure." Mia followed him inside. "What needs to be done?"

"Feeding. Watering. Cleaning. The usual stuff. But first you should come with me to check on the nursery."

The word "nursery" made Mia think of a fancy hospital room with rows of babies, but this one was a greenhouse sort of tent in the corner of the warehouse. Daniel unzipped the flap and held it while Mia stepped inside. It was even warmer than the cricket room and muggy.

"Oh, excellent!" Daniel looked into a bin on the shelf. "We have pinheads!"

The box was full of tiny, pale baby crickets. They looked like the little white heads on the pins Mia's other grandmother used for sewing.

Daniel handed the box to Mia, lifted the nursery tent flap, and pointed to one of the bins. "Want to dump them into their new home?"

Mia did that while Daniel opened a big bag of chicken feed. "So now we'll grind up some fresh feed and then— Oh no!"

Mia rushed over. The feed was crawling with coppery-colored beetles.

Daniel crumpled the top of the bag closed and picked it up. He jerked his head toward the lobby. "Open the door!"

Mia raced over and opened it, and Daniel ran straight through. He tripped over Syd, who yelped indignantly, but Daniel didn't stop until he was across the parking lot. He flopped the bag down in the grass with a thump.

"What are they?" Mia asked.

"Maybe mealworm beetles?" Daniel said, catching his breath. "But that feed was fine yesterday."

Mia's heart raced. Could Gram be right about that guy trying to sabotage her farm? "Do you think somebody *put* them in there?"

Daniel shrugged. "It's messed up, but I don't see how else this could happen. I was thinking that our temperature and humidity issues last month could have been technical glitches. And the seagulls were just weird. But now . . ." He shook his head. "Those beetles could be carrying ten kinds of diseases. If I'd dumped that feed in with the crickets . . ." He looked at Mia. "We're going to have to keep a closer eye on this place. Because if she's right—if somebody *is* trying to sabotage the farm—this could be just the beginning."

CHAPTER 6

Who's a Warrior?

Mia helped Daniel open a new bag of beetle-free feed and get the crickets fed, and then it was time for Warrior Camp. The businesses in Gram's warehouse all had their own doors to the outside, but there was also a long inside hallway that connected them. Mia didn't feel like going back out into the sun, so she went that way. She hadn't realized at first how big the whole warehouse was; Gram's farm and Green Mountain Moose each took up about a fifth of the huge space, and the rest was the big gym Mia had seen on her first day. It was divided into two sections—the Warrior Camp training center and a traditional gymnastics place with all the equipment.

Mia stepped inside and froze. Just walking into a gym

again made her throat feel dry and tight. She'd only agreed to this so she could spend time with Gram.

It's okay, she told herself. This wasn't gymnastics. She was going to be a warrior. She'd give it a try, and if nothing else, she'd learn a few secrets from the show.

But in order to get to Warrior Camp, Mia had to walk past the gymnastics center. It had a big window so families could watch. Mia looked through the glass. A girl had just done a tuck jump on the balance beam, and she was wobbling. It made Mia's insides wobbly, too. She looked away.

"Are you here for gymnastics camp?" a tall woman in a tracksuit asked.

"No!" Mia answered, a little too loud. "Sorry. I mean . . . I used to do gymnastics, but I'm in Warrior Camp this summer."

"I thought you looked like a gymnast!" the lady said. Her hair was tucked into a bun, and she had a friendly smile. "Well, you'll love Maria and Joe at Warrior Camp." She pointed to a red door on the other side of the lobby. "But if you decide to do gymnastics, too, we have classes all summer. I'm Jamie, and you can ask for me, okay?"

"Thanks," Mia said. *But no thanks*, she thought, and headed for the red door. She couldn't help looking through the window again, though. Now another girl was on the beam, teetering as she got ready to do a back walkover.

Mia's hand went to her arm. She trailed a finger along the scar from her surgery, and her heart sped up. There were balance-beam sorts of challenges on the warrior show she watched sometimes. She hoped they wouldn't have those at camp.

Mia walked up to the red door and took a deep breath. Camp only lasted two hours. She'd be fine.

"Are you a warrior or what?" someone asked from behind her.

Mia turned and saw a freckly little girl in gym shorts and a bright pink tank top. She looked like she might be eight or nine. "Sorry." Mia stepped aside. "I'm here for camp, but you can go ahead."

The girl put her hands on her hips and looked Mia up and down. "You look scared," she announced, "but you shouldn't be, because it's fun and everything is super easy once you get the hang of it and we get watermelon for snack most days. So are you coming?" The girl was holding the door, so Mia went in.

At first, it was cool to see the equipment from the show, but within seconds, Mia felt overwhelmed. There were so many kids! And they were shouting about their favorite equipment all at once.

"Whoa! The jumping spider!"

"The warped wall! Cool!"

Most were younger than Mia, which made her feel a little embarrassed but also a little better. At least there wouldn't be anybody her own age to make fun of her.

The space was small, but it seemed like every single challenge from the TV show was squeezed in there. The freckly girl from the door had already scrambled up a rock wall and made it halfway across a monkey-bars thing. Two boys were taking turns running up the warped wall and sliding back down.

"I got to ten feet that time!" one shouted.

"Did not! Your fingers didn't touch the line!"

There were a dozen kids climbing ladders and poles, shimmying along pipes that hung from the ceiling, and bouncing on mini-trampolines. It felt loud and chaotic and dangerous. Mia wondered if she could sneak back out to the cricket farm before anyone noticed.

"Welcome to Warrior Camp!" a tall woman with a blue buzz cut called from one corner of the gym. She was standing next to a shorter guy with a frizzy ponytail, and they both had totally ripped muscles like the people on the show. "Let's sit in a circle so we can stretch!"

When everyone had settled in, the blue-haired coach shouted, "Who's a warrior?"

"We are!" everybody except Mia shouted back. It was starting to feel like Launch Camp, like they'd all been here before, and Mia couldn't help thinking that she should have looked more carefully at those brochures. Knitting Camp, for example, was sounding better by the minute.

"That's great!" the coach said. "I'm Maria, and this is Joe." The ponytail guy waved. "We're your coaches, and we know most of you. But who's new this session?" Everybody looked at Mia, so she raised her hand.

Then the door opened, and Clover came flying in, blond curls bouncing off her shoulders. "Sorry I'm late!"

Mia waved, and Clover's face lit up. She hurried over and plopped down beside her.

"Have you done this before?" Mia whispered while Maria was going over rules.

Clover shook her head. "My moms made me come. They said I had to do at least two activities this summer."

"Same," Mia said, and felt a little better about this one.

They went around the circle to introduce themselves, which confirmed that Mia and Clover were the oldest. Isaac and Liam were eight-year-old twins. Luke, Andy, and Matt were all nine. Ally, Emma, Jake, and Amir were ten. TJ was eleven, and Carlee, the freckly girl Mia had met on her way in, was seven.

"We'll start with some stretching," Maria said. "Spread out and roll your shoulders."

Clover wiggled herself closer to Mia. "How's your business plan going?" she whispered.

"Let's stretch our legs now! Spread them out and walk your hands forward . . ."

Mia stretched. "The plan's okay, but my gram's cricket farm is kind of a mess. She thinks—" Mia stopped. She really didn't know Clover and wasn't sure how much to share. But Clover seemed smart. Maybe she'd have ideas. "She thinks somebody is trying to sabotage her farm."

"Take a deep breath and see if you can get forward a little more," Maria said. "Look at Carlee!"

Mia looked. Carlee was leaned over with her chest and stomach flat on the floor, her skinny legs spread almost in a split. Mia used to be flexible like that. Before she got hurt and everything.

Mia stretched a little more, leaned toward Clover, and whispered what had happened—how that guy had tried to buy Gram's farm but she said no. And then the seagulls showed up. And then the beetles.

"Whoa." Clover leaned to stretch the other way. "Sure sounds like somebody's messing with her."

"Now reach for your toes!" Maria called.

Mia reached. "I know, right? But we can't call the police just because we *think* that guy might be doing stuff."

"We need to find evidence!" Clover said. "I'll help. I love mysteries. My moms still have their whole Nancy Drew collections from when they were little. I read a few, and they weren't the greatest, but there are way better mysteries out there now. Have you read *The Parker Inheritance*? Or *Moxie and the Art of Rule Breaking*? Or *Me, Frida, and the Secret of the Peacock Ring*?"

Mia shook her head.

"Point your toes and stretch again!" Maria called.

"Well, they're amazing, and you should read them," Clover said. "Plus, it'll give us ideas for how to investigate the sabotage at your grandmother's farm. But I have some thoughts already. We can start after camp!"

Mia was about to ask Clover what those thoughts were when Joe shouted from across the room. "Over here, everybody!"

He was standing near a line of rings hanging from the ceiling. The twins ran over, and one of them—Isaac or Liam, Mia couldn't tell them apart—jumped up and swung across. Joe gave a big whoop and turned to Mia. "You're up next. Ready?"

She wasn't. But she nodded anyway and jumped up to grab the rings. Then she just sort of dangled.

"Pull on the back ring so you get a swing going," Joe said.

Mia tried to do that, but it felt like her arms might pull out of their sockets.

"Here . . . want me to give you a little extra swing?"

Joe held up his hands as if he were getting ready to spot her, but he waited for Mia to answer.

She didn't. Her heart sped up. She didn't want help, and she didn't want anybody to touch her. *No,* she thought. But her throat went dry, and she couldn't say it. She couldn't say anything. Even her breath felt trapped. Her arms were burning, and now her eyes were, too. She let go and dropped to the mat. Hot tears spilled down her cheeks. Now everyone at Warrior Camp would think she was a terrible sport.

"Hey . . . it's okay." Joe followed Mia off the mats as Jake jumped up to the rings. "You want to try again?"

Mia looked at him and swallowed hard. He seemed so nice, like he truly wanted to help her. But you really didn't know anything at all about a person just because they seemed nice.

Mia shook her head and said, "I can't do this. I broke my arm, like, really bad, a while ago, and I . . . I just can't."

"Ohh . . ." Joe nodded. "Bummer."

Mia nodded. It really was. The broken arm and everything else.

"I broke mine rock climbing three years ago," Joe said. "It was brutal trying to get back into things. First day I went to the gym, I had this dull, aching pain right here." He rubbed his forearm.

It was where Mia's arm hurt, too. She nodded. "I thought I could do this, but it's too much."

"We'll get you back up there," Joe said, "but for now, let's try something else." He led her to a hanging bar that was set apart from the other challenges. "Whenever you're ready, just hop up there and see how long you can hang."

Mia took a shaky breath and jumped. She grabbed the bar with both hands and held on, swaying back and forth. She couldn't believe how soon her muscles started burning. She used to do three-minute routines on the uneven bars, swinging the whole time and pulling herself up to the higher bar, over and over. She used to be so strong.

She tried to count seconds in her head but only made it to six before she had to let go. Tears stung her eyes again.

"That was great!" Joe said, as if she'd just made it through an entire warrior course in record time. "You want to give the spider wall a try now?"

Mia blinked away her tears and looked across the room to where kids were leaping off a little trampoline and sticking—somehow—with their hands and feet on two walls about four feet apart. If she couldn't even hold on to a dumb bar for ten seconds, there was no way she'd be able to do that. But she was trapped here for—what—another half hour at least? Mia's heart started racing again, as if it were trying to bust out of her chest and leave without her.

Why couldn't she feel normal and try things like everyone else?

"No pressure," Joe said. "Maybe you just want to work on building some arm strength on the bar today?"

Mia nodded, and Joe started to leave, but then he turned back to Mia. "Hey. You know, it's okay to come back slowly after an injury like this. You just need to stretch. When that bone in your arm was healing, your muscles and tendons and everything tightened up around it to protect it."

Mia looked down at her scar. It wasn't just her arm that felt that way. It was all of her. And it was hard to believe that any amount of stretching could fix that.

CHAPTER 7

Chocolate Cricket Cookie Dough

The best thing about Warrior Camp was that it made Launch Camp feel like a vacation. Mia woke up Wednesday with both forearms aching but happy she wouldn't have to hang from anything all day. She also woke up thinking about her business plan and decided to bring a jar of Gram's sea salt and garlic crickets to camp.

Mia had been thinking about what Zoya said, about creating demand by convincing people to eat crickets. For years, Gram had been all about sneaking cricket powder into cookies and smoothies for extra protein. But when you ran an actual business, you couldn't do that. You had to tell the truth about ingredients, especially since people who were allergic to shellfish might also be allergic to insects. They had to find a way to get more people to eat crickets on purpose. And tasting them was the first step.

When Mia got to camp, she brought the crickets to Clover, who popped a handful into her mouth, no problem. "They taste like salty potato chips or corn nuts," she said as she chewed. "And maybe a tiny bit like dirt."

Mia laughed. "I'm not sure that's a great selling point."

"We have to find the right way to say it." Clover helped herself to a few more. "A crunchy, nutty, earthy snack!"

"Did somebody say snack?" Eli slid his chair over.

"Yep." Mia held out the jar. "Want a roasted cricket?"

"Seriously?" Eli looked into the container and hesitated.

"These are sea salt and garlic," Mia said, and tossed a few in her mouth. "The maple ones are good, too."

"Maple crickets?" Eli said, loudly enough that Dylan rode his skateboard across the room to see what was going on. Pretty soon, half the camp was snacking on crickets. Anna and Quan and Julia said they were pretty good. Aidan tasted one but wasn't wild about it. Dylan was allergic to shellfish, so he couldn't try one, and Bella said there was no way she was eating a bug on purpose. Eli took one but then just kept staring at it.

"Dude, it's only a bug," Clover said. "It's protein!"

"Protein with legs." Eli wrinkled his nose. "But okay. I'm gonna do this." He made a big show of holding it with two fingers and smiled a big dimply smile. "Somebody get a picture!"

Quan took a photo, and then Eli popped the cricket into his mouth. "Not my favorite," he said. "But send me that picture, okay? I want to share it. It'll freak people out."

"Take a picture of me eating one, too!" Julia said, and posed the same way.

Aidan must have decided he liked attention more than he didn't like crickets. He ate another one so Quan could take his picture, too.

"Are you posting yours now?" Eli asked, poking at his phone. "We need a hashtag."

"Yes!" Clover turned to Mia. Her eyes were huge. "That's exactly what we need! Eli didn't want to try a cricket, but everybody else was into it, and then it seemed cool, so he not only wanted to try one, he wanted to *show* everybody he did. It's perfect!"

Mia nodded slowly. "You think this could happen on a bigger scale?"

"Totally," Clover said. "My mom works in marketing and always says a hashtag is a great way to get people talking. Everyone will want to try it!"

"Yeah!" Eli was all into the crickets now. "The eat-an-insect challenge."

"The Chirp Challenge!" Mia said, clapping her hands.

"That's it! We'll make a big banner." Clover jumped on a chair and held the imaginary banner in her arms. "Hashtag: Chirp Challenge!" She turned to Mia. "Where can we set this up?"

Mia knew the answer right away. But she'd already said no to staffing Gram's booth at the farmers market. She had never liked talking to strangers to begin with. The only time she'd ever felt comfortable out in front of people was when she was doing gymnastics, flying over the bars or tumbling across the floor. Now that she didn't have that, it was harder to think about being brave somewhere else.

But maybe it wasn't too late to change her mind about the market. Mia imagined herself standing with Clover at the booth in City Hall Park, handing out samples and telling people about the Chirp Challenge. Somehow, the idea of sharing roasted crickets with strangers seemed less scary with Clover by her side.

At lunchtime, Mia texted Mom, who said it was fine if she and Clover worked at the market for Gram a week from Saturday. Next, Mia texted Gram, who replied with ten cricket emojis. Mia hurried over to tell Clover it was a go.

"Perfect!" Clover said. "I'll help you make a whole social media campaign."

"That'd be great," Mia said, "but aren't you doing KicksFinder?"

Clover shrugged. "My part is pretty much done. Nick

and Eli are just debugging now. They don't need me until the competition. Also, I'd rather work with you. Because we need to talk about your gram's sabotage situation, too. I was rereading this book *To Catch a Cheat* last night, and I have an idea for how we can scope out that guy she doesn't like."

"You mean, like, *spy* on him?"

"Kind of. We can talk about that later. And oh! You know what else I was thinking?"

Mia shook her head. Clover's brain changed gears so fast it was hard to keep up.

"When we're downtown for the market, we should visit businesses and ask if they'll add crickets to their menus. Didn't you say some restaurants already do that?"

"Not here, but yeah."

"I bet we could get some bars to offer bowls of roasted crickets instead of nuts or pretzels. And what about on pizza?"

"Yes!" Mia found her business plan so she could get all these ideas down. "That chocolate shop on Church Street could do chocolate-covered crickets. And the ice-cream place could use them as mix-ins!"

Mia had been half-joking about that last one, but Clover was already naming flavors. "Chocolate Cricket Cookie Dough!"

"Mint Chocolate Chirp!"

"Mealworm Marshmallow!"

Mia wrinkled her nose. "Let's stick to crickets for now."

"Fair enough." Clover put on a more serious face. "We have a lot of work to do over the next week and a half. I'll make the banner. You should get your pitch ready for the restaurants."

"My pitch?" Somehow, Mia hadn't thought about the fact that all these fun ideas had to be shared. Out loud. With strangers. But Clover was so enthusiastic that Mia would feel like a jerk if she bailed out now. "Okay," she said. "Let's get to work!"

CHAPTER 8

A Bark in the Dark

Mia spent Wednesday night in her room, trying to figure out what to say to strangers who might want to serve crickets in their restaurants but probably not.

"Crickets are the superfood of tomorrow," she practiced in her mirror. "Trendy restaurants across the globe are already serving insects on everything from tacos to avocado toast." She ran through the pitch again and again until she could almost imagine saying it to strangers without getting queasy.

She practiced some more at Launch Camp on Thursday, while Clover worked on the Chirp Challenge banner.

"We hope you'll consider leading the way in what's sure to be a food revolution!"

"Perfect!" Clover put down her paintbrush and applauded.

"Yeah, but it's easy with you guys. You're not strangers." As soon as Mia said that, she realized how great it was—that somehow her fellow Launch Campers already felt like friends. It wasn't like they even talked outside their teams that much. But everybody was kind of in tune with everybody else. People were always stopping to check out Dylan and Julia's soda-can-tab earrings and sample Quan and Bella's dumplings or Aidan's cookies. Eli made sure everybody knew when he and Nick made progress on KicksFinder, and even though Anna was quiet, she ran a demonstration of her robot arm, and everybody cheered when it managed to pick up a pencil and put it in the electric sharpener. It felt good to be working together in that room, even though they were working on different things.

At the end of the morning, Clover rolled up the banner. "So listen. I have some ideas for gathering intel on that Chet Potsworth guy." She pulled a notebook from her backpack. "I was doing some research online, and his food-processing plant—Nature's Healthy Harvest, it's called—is less than half a mile from the cricket farm. We should take a walk and check things out before camp today."

"Check what things out?" Mia asked as they unlocked their bikes. "It's not like we can knock on the door and ask if he's hiding seagulls and beetles in there."

"No, but we can go in and have a look around," Clover said. They hopped on their bikes and started down the path. It was almost eighty degrees, but Lake Champlain hadn't warmed up yet, so a cool breeze blew in from the water.

"Even if they'd let us in, I can't imagine we'd learn much," Mia said, swerving around a fallen tree branch.

"I wouldn't be so sure." Clover stood on her pedals to catch up. "In my books, there are always clues around—papers and open emails and stuff. Criminals can be pretty dumb. We should check it out, at least."

"Maybe. If Gram doesn't need help." Mia hoped that Gram would need help. She didn't think she'd be as good at sleuthing as the characters in Clover's mysteries.

"Oh! I love this park!" Clover pulled her bike over to the side of the path and took out her phone. Mia recognized the little beach right away. It was the one where she'd jumped off the high rocks into the water. The one from the picture. The sky was impossibly blue today, too, and the rocks were still that perfect red. But Mia couldn't imagine herself jumping from them now. She didn't feel like a person who got to do things like that anymore.

Clover was that kind of person, though. Mia watched her balance on a rock for a selfie, and she felt envious. As they rode the rest of the way out to the farm, Mia decided she should at least try to be more that way. Like Clover.

Like she used to be. The kind of person who wasn't afraid to jump off rocks and try things.

Because what if they *could* learn something to keep Chet Potsworth from messing with Gram's farm? What if they could make a difference with the Chirp Challenge and outreach to local businesses? What if Mia could do more than she thought? She owed it to Gram to try.

When they got to the farm, Syd came wobbling out to greet them, wagging her stub of a tail. When she saw Clover, she stopped and barked like an attack dog.

"Wow. Your dog hates me," Clover said.

"Syd hates everyone for fifteen seconds or so. After that, she's your best friend. See?"

Syd was already nuzzling Clover's shins, looking for love.

"Well, you're a pushover, aren't you?" Clover bent down to rub Syd's belly.

"Hey, I'm glad you're here." Daniel came out of the office. "We got to the bottom of one of our issues, at least. Bob helped me rewire the humidifiers so we don't keep blowing fuses." He gestured to another man who was walking out of the office with Gram.

"Well, hello there!" he said.

It was the Moose Man Mia had met on Saturday. She almost called him that but caught herself and remembered to be polite. "Hi. It's nice to see you again."

He smiled at Mia. "You know, I found out you were being humble when you said you didn't play a sport. Your grandmother says you're quite the gymnast."

"Not anymore," Mia said quickly.

Thankfully, Daniel rescued her from the Moose Man. "Mia, how would you and your pal feel about cleaning out water dishes?"

"Sure." Mia and Clover followed him into the cricket room.

"It's so loud in here!" Clover said.

"Yep," Mia said. "Whoever made up that phrase 'nothing but crickets' to describe silence has never been in a room with a million chirping crickets."

"More like half a million," Daniel said. "Only the males chirp."

"Wait, what?" Mia had never known that. "Female crickets don't chirp?"

Daniel shook his head. "Just males. To get attention when they're looking to mate. Also to show other males how tough they are. But the females don't make any noises at all."

"I bet they're secretly in charge of everything," Clover said.

Daniel laughed. "I wouldn't doubt that."

Mia laughed, too, but when she looked into the bin, she couldn't help wondering about all those quiet females.

Was it that they couldn't chirp at all, no matter what? Or were the boy crickets so loud that they never got the chance? It felt like too weird a question to ask, so Mia stayed quiet, too.

"Hey, are you on the baseball team?" Clover asked, pointing to Daniel's Lake Monsters hat.

"I am!" he said. "Need tickets for a game?"

"No, but we have an idea for the concession stand." Clover looked at Mia and grinned.

"I read that the Seattle Mariners are selling toasted grasshoppers at their games," Mia said. "And they keep selling out! So maybe the Lake Monsters could try that, too. With crickets."

"That's a great idea. I'll ask—but if we do that, we're going to need more crickets, so let's get to work."

Mia and Clover chose a bin and reached in for the water dishes.

"Why is that one white?" Clover pointed into the cricket cubbies, where a pale-white cricket was tucked away, clinging to the cardboard.

"Probably just molted," Daniel said, "so it'll be hiding out for a bit. When crickets shed their old exoskeletons, their bodies are soft for a little while, so they're extra vulnerable. The other crickets know that and take the opportunity to come after them."

"Sounds like middle school," said Clover.

Or gymnastics, Mia thought. She couldn't look away from that poor cowering cricket. "How long does it last?"

"Just a few hours," Daniel said. "That cricket will be good as new before we leave tonight." His phone rang then, and he looked kind of alarmed. "I . . . uh . . . need to take this," he said, and hurried out the back door.

"Everything okay?" Mia asked when he got back.

"Yeah." Daniel glanced at the door to the lobby, then looked back at Mia and Clover. "It was nothing, really. Did you finish with the water?"

Mia nodded, and Daniel asked them to handle the feed, too, while he made another phone call.

"That's a little shady," Clover said as Mia poured feed into a dish.

"What?"

"Daniel being all secret about his phone call. Who do you think he's talking to?"

"I don't know. James?" Mia lowered the dish into one of the cricket bins.

"I just think he's acting weird," Clover said. When Daniel came back, he set his phone on a counter and started cleaning up one of the bins.

"We're out of feed over here!" Clover called as she poured the last of her bag into a dish.

"I'll run out back to get more," Daniel said. As soon as

he walked out, his phone dinged with a text. Clover ran over and picked it up.

"Clover!" Mia's heart raced. "He's coming right back!"

"Look at this!" Clover motioned her over. Mia ran up the row of cricket bins and looked down at the phone. The text was from a contact Daniel had named "Ron at Agri-Corps," and it said: *Great. We'll see you at 4:30 today for the interview!*

"He's interviewing for another job!" Clover said. "What if he's—"

"Shh!" Mia heard the door opening and pulled Clover away from the phone.

"Here you go!" Daniel dropped the feed on the floor and looked at his watch. "But don't you need to get going for camp? I have to leave by four, but I can finish with the food."

"Okay." Mia's mind was racing. "Do you have . . . uh . . . a game or something?" She wondered if he'd tell the truth.

"Uh . . . no," Daniel said. "Just an appointment thing."

"Oh." Mia stared at him until Clover nudged her. "Well yeah, we should go. We're already kind of late."

"Why would he be applying for a job?" Clover said as they hurried down the hall to Warrior Camp. "And trying to keep it a secret?"

"I don't know," Mia said. "He's supposed to be Gram's friend. How can he just abandon her with so much going wrong?"

"Maybe he's the reason things keep going wrong," Clover said. "What if he's working with that Potsworth guy? We need to keep an eye on him."

When they got to Warrior Camp, Maria was already demonstrating an obstacle called the quad steps, a row of staggered ramps where you had to jump from one to the next.

"There are a few strategies for this obstacle," Maria said. "There's the cat." She demonstrated, jumping onto the first step, grabbing the top edge, and crouching low before jumping to the next. "You can do twinkle toes and take three quick steps each time." Maria twinkle-toed her way back. "Or there's the stride, which looks like this." This time, she just ran from step to step with big, long bounds. "Line up and you can try whatever feels best to you."

Mia thought that was sort of like saying, "You can get stung by a bee, punched in the nose, or poked with a sharp stick—whatever feels best," but she sighed and got in line. As soon as she did, her heart thumped faster. What if she lost her balance and fell off one of those ramps? What if she landed on the same arm she broke before?

"I don't think I'm ready for this one," she told Maria when it was her turn.

"Oh no, you'll be fine," Maria said. "This doesn't require arm strength. It's about balance."

That was the problem, but Mia couldn't say so without explaining things she didn't want to explain, so she took a deep breath and forced herself to jump toward the first ramp. She slid down as soon as she landed.

"Wipe the bottom of your sneakers and try again," Maria said.

Mia didn't want to try again. But everyone was staring, waiting for her to do something. She felt like a molting cricket.

"Try it," Maria said. "It'll help you get a grip."

Right, Mia thought. *Get a grip*. She wiped off her shoes and jumped onto the step again. It actually helped. This time, Mia made it through the first three steps. But when she leaped for the fourth step, she missed. The edge of the wood scraped a bunch of skin off her leg.

"Ow!" She limped off to the side, rubbing her shin.

"Ah . . . battle scars," Joe said. "All warriors have battle scars. Want to give it one more try?"

"Not right now." Or ever. Mia traced the pink scar on her arm. She had enough battle scars, thanks. But she knew Joe and Maria would want her to do something, so she went back to her strengthen-the-arms hang. Her shin still hurt, but this time, she stayed on the bar for eleven seconds before she dropped.

"Good job! You're already getting stronger!" Joe shouted from the rings. He was helping Amir, who'd made it through the first five rings but got stuck because the last one was farther away.

"I can't get that one," Amir said, dangling, as Mia jumped back up to her bar.

"Sure you can!" Joe said. "Big swing!"

Amir swung and touched it but couldn't get a grip.

Joe clapped anyway. "You touched it! And you're still holding on!"

Mia was still holding on, too. And that was something. She'd been watching Amir instead of counting seconds, but she guessed it was at least fifteen before she had to drop.

Amir was swinging all over the place now, and Mia thought he'd have to start over. But instead, he reached back to the ring behind him, held it until he was stable, and then finished.

"Great!" Joe turned to the kids who were waiting. "Did you see how when Amir's swing got all wild, he went back to the ring before? You can steady yourself that way. By reaching back." He looked over at Mia then. "You ready to give these rings a try?"

"Not yet. But maybe next time," she said, and jumped up for one more arm hang.

"You did great on the spider wall today," Mia told Clover as they left. Mia had agreed to ride over to the food-processing plant to see if they could get inside without it being weird.

"Thanks," Clover said as they walked down the hall. "I finally figured out—" She stopped, and as soon as she did, Mia heard a dog barking. "Is that Syd?" Clover asked. They raced to the cricket farm door.

"Locked." Clover looked up at the high window above the door. "And it's dark in there."

Mia nodded. "Everybody's gone, remember? That's why we had to bring all our stuff to Warrior Camp." Daniel had left for his "just an appointment," and Gram had told them she was leaving Syd in the office while she ran out to meet with a maybe-investor.

"Then why is the dog so upset?" Clover whispered just as the barking stopped. There was a shuffling sound on the other side of the door. And then voices.

Had Daniel or Gram come back? Mia pressed her ear to the door.

"Hurry up!" a gruff voice said. It didn't sound like Daniel. "Not there. Out of sight."

"Where's that flashlight?"

"How's this?"

And then something that sounded like "mess in the morning."

"Someone's in there!" Mia hissed.

It got quiet for a few seconds. Then one of the voices came through the door loud and clear. "All right! Let's get out of here." Whoever it was had to be just on the other side!

Mia grabbed Clover's hand and ran down the hallway. Whoever was in there didn't sound like friends. What if it was Chet Potsworth, sabotaging the farm again with some other awful man? What if they caught Mia and Clover spying on them?

Mia burst out the door to the parking lot, pulling Clover behind her, and ran to their bikes. Clover had locked hers, so she had to fiddle with the combination.

"Hurry!" Mia looked back at the warehouse. No one had come out yet, but they had to be on their way.

"Got it!" Clover yanked the lock off her bike. Her face was all red and sweaty. "Let's go!" And she took off.

Mia jumped on her bike, stood, and pedaled as hard as she could. She didn't know who she'd heard on the other side of that door, but she felt sure of one thing. They were doing something bad. They must have thought they were alone.

What would they do if they found out they weren't?

CHAPTER 9

Uninvited Guests

Mia's legs burned. Her heart thudded in her ears as they tore out of the industrial park, down the street, and back onto the bike path. They pedaled all the way home and skidded into Mia's driveway as her mom was getting out of the car with groceries.

"Mom!" Mia called, then bent over because she was wheezing too much to talk.

Her mom looked up and frowned. "You look exhausted! Did you forget to hydrate at Warrior Camp?"

Clover caught her breath first. "We rode back really fast because we heard somebody at the cricket farm."

"Somebody broke in, Mom!" Mia blurted out, still panting. "We have to call the police!" As soon as Mia said that, she wondered why she hadn't done it already. She had a phone. That's what she should have done as soon as they got outside. But when you were freaking out about bad guys on the other side of a door, you didn't think about those things.

"Hold on." Mom put the groceries down on a porch step. *"What's* going on?"

"We heard them!" Mia said. "Daniel and Gram were gone, but we heard voices when we were walking past the door after Warrior Camp. Somebody else was in there! And they said—" What was it they'd said? "Something about a mess."

"What's a mess? The farm?" Mom looked confused.

"I guess?" Mia was suddenly second-guessing herself.

"Are you sure it wasn't Daniel? Maybe he forgot something."

"I mean . . . maybe?" It hadn't sounded like Daniel, but there had been a big door between them. "But there were two voices. Plus Syd was barking, and she only ever barks at strangers."

Mom thought about that. "Well, maybe he had a friend with him, right? I'm sure it's fine, but I'll call Gram and let her know what happened." She turned to Clover. "Do you want to stay for dinner?"

Clover shook her head. "Thanks, but I have to get

home." She looked at Mia. "Let me know if you hear anything, okay?"

Mia nodded and went inside. She tried to put the groceries away quietly so she could eavesdrop while Mom called Gram from the living room.

"They said they heard voices . . .

"She's not sure.

"So you didn't see anything?

"And it's all good?

"Great. We'll see you tomorrow night for the fireworks.

"Right. Okay . . . Bye."

Mom came back into the kitchen and picked up a package of chicken thighs. "Gram's already back at the farm. She says Syd is quiet and happy, and nothing is out of place. She thinks you might have heard the building owner. He'd mentioned he was going to stop by to look at something with the electricity."

"Okay," Mia said. But no matter what Gram said, it didn't *feel* like everything was okay. She went up to her room, took a shower, put a bandage on her scraped-up shin, and changed into sweatpants and a comfy T-shirt. Then she flopped down on her bed with Neptune.

Mia's quad-steps battle scar still stung, her arms were sore from warrior hanging, and her brain was spinning.

Had she and Clover heard a burglar at the farm? Or had she worked herself up over nothing? What if it *was* Daniel, and he was involved in the sabotage somehow?

Mia stroked Neptune's velvety fins and wished she could go back to being eight. Back to the girl in the picture, who'd jumped so fearlessly off those red rocks. She never used to be afraid of things. She used to be so sure of herself, and now she didn't feel sure of anything.

Mia rolled off the bed, pulled one of the boxes from her closet, and rummaged through until she found the photo. She didn't know why, but she needed to hold it.

It was funny. She looked so tiny in that lake rocks picture, but she hadn't felt that way. Even though she was older and taller now, she felt smaller somehow. As if her body was growing like it was supposed to, but inside, the rest of her was shrinking.

"Mia!" Mom's voice came up from the kitchen. "Would you set the table, please?"

"Coming!"

Mia looked down at the picture in her hands. Maybe it would be like the rings at Warrior Camp. Maybe reaching back to that old version of herself, and holding on for a minute or two, could steady the Mia she was now. She put the picture up next to her mirror and shoved the box back into her closet.

She wasn't ready to unpack the other memories buried under her old homework and gymnastics medals. Not yet.

On Friday morning, Gram called, so upset that Dad couldn't understand what she was saying. She was at the cricket farm, so he and Mia drove out to meet her.

"I don't understand," Dad said on the way. "Last night, she told Mom everything was fine."

It wasn't fine anymore. As soon as they turned into the parking lot, they saw Daniel hop out of his car with a cloth insect net and race inside. Mia and Dad followed him. Mr. Jacobson the Moose Man was there, too, trying to get Gram to calm down. She wasn't calming, though.

"Don't tell me it's fine! How am I supposed to get rid of ten million fruit flies?"

"Fruit flies?" Dad asked.

"Ten *million*?" Mia said.

"Give or take," Mr. Jacobson said, nodding toward the cricket room. "It's a mess in there."

Mia turned to Gram. "But I thought everything was fine last night."

"They hadn't hatched yet," she said.

"Whoever you heard in there must have hidden the pupae," Daniel explained, "knowing the flies would emerge overnight. And boy, did they. Take a look."

Mia peered through the window in the door. Clouds of fruit flies swarmed above the cricket bins. It reminded Mia of the time she'd left a banana in her locker over April break but times a million. "They're everywhere!"

"Yeah," Daniel said, looking down at the net in his hands. "It's kind of hopeless." Mia searched his face for signs that he might be involved in the fruit-fly mess somehow, but he seemed genuinely upset. Some people were good at faking, though. She knew that.

"It most certainly is not hopeless!" Gram pointed her finger at Daniel's chest. "You go to the hardware store and buy all the glue traps they have." She whirled around to Mia. "You can go in there and remove the substrate." When Mia looked confused, Gram added, "Those dishes of dirt where the crickets lay eggs. I don't want those nasty flies reproducing."

"But what about your cricket eggs?" Mr. Jacobson asked. "Maybe you should wait and—"

"Nope." Gram shook her head. "We'll have to lose this generation. We have to stop those flies from reproducing." She started for her office. "I'm going to report this to the police."

"I think we have some glue traps at home, too." Dad

looked at Mia. "I'll go pick them up if you're okay here for a while."

Mia nodded and headed into the cricket room. One by one, she picked up the little dishes of dirt where the crickets laid their eggs. She wondered how many fruit-fly eggs were already in there. She'd been so scared when she heard those voices yesterday, but now, she felt a surge of anger. What kind of a person would do something like this? She wished she and Clover had seen whoever it was.

Mia was changing the crickets' water when Daniel came back with glue traps. "We need to find out who did this," she said.

Daniel sighed as he unloaded the bag. "Honestly, I'm not sure it matters at this point."

Mia stared at him. If Daniel didn't want them to find out, there could be only one reason. But she asked, "Why doesn't it matter?"

Daniel stepped up on a chair, hung the sticky trap from a beam, and sighed. "Raising crickets is challenging even when things go well. Fruit flies aside, we can't seem to get this place to the point where it's sustainable. Everything takes too long." He gestured toward the water dishes in the sink. "Cleaning and feeding and watering, and especially the harvest."

He seemed honestly frustrated again, which made Mia think he probably wasn't involved in the fruit-fly situation.

Also, she was surprised that the harvest was a problem. That had always seemed pretty simple to her. "Don't you just shake the crickets off their cardboard cubbies and put them in the freezer?" Gram always talked about how humane it was to harvest crickets. When you put them in the freezer, they went to sleep, which is what crickets do in nature when it gets cold.

"Nope. If you did that, you'd accidentally harvest some crickets that are already dead, and that's kind of gross. So we have to take each cardboard condo, shake all the crickets off into a plastic bin, and then put the condo down and wait for them to climb back up. Those crickets are obviously alive, so they can be harvested. But they don't all climb up right away, so you have to do it over and over." Daniel looked at his watch. "We only have one bin to harvest, but it'll take me until noon, at least." His phone dinged with a text, and he turned away to reply.

Mia watched him reply to whoever it was. Maybe Daniel was looking at new jobs because he was worried the farm might fail. She couldn't really blame him for that, given how things were going. The guy needed a job. But until he knew for sure, he might keep it a secret so Gram wouldn't think he was giving up on her. Still, it was kind of a crummy thing to do. But maybe if Gram got her investors and things got better, Daniel would stay, and everything would be fine. All Mia could do was keep helping as much as she could.

She finished changing the water and added feed to the dishes while Daniel started the harvest. It really did look like a pain in the neck. He'd shake crickets off, wait for them to climb back up, and then shake those into a different bin to be harvested. Then he'd put the cricket condo back in the first bin and wait for more live crickets to climb on. He looked like a robot. Back and forth. Shake and wait. And that gave Mia an idea. She'd seen Anna's robot arm pick up pencils and ping-pong balls and swivel to drop them into buckets. Why couldn't it pick up cricket condos, too?

CHAPTER 10

The First Firefly of Summer

Mia thought about that the whole drive home. She and Dad had to stop for some errands, so by the time they walked through the door, Mom was already packing the cooler for their fireworks picnic.

"Does Clover want a ride tonight?" Mom asked.

"No, she's riding bikes there with her moms, so they'll meet us."

After Mia changed her clothes, they drove to pick up Gram, who was surprisingly chipper, given her fruit-fly infestation.

Mia almost didn't want to ask, but she was too curious. "How's everything at the farm?"

"Buggy," Gram said, and waved her hand in front of her face as if she were swatting fruit flies. "But let's not talk about that tonight. I'm going to enjoy the fireworks with my granddaughter."

"Hey! They're playing my song!" Dad turned up the radio. It was tuned to the country station that played "God Bless the U.S.A." practically nonstop on Independence Day weekend. Dad sang along every time. Badly. By the time the song ended, they were all laughing.

"I'll drop you off and find a spot," Dad said as they pulled up to the waterfront. Mia knew he was doing that so Gram wouldn't have to walk far with her droopy foot, but Dad was smart enough to add "because the cooler's heavy" so she wouldn't argue.

The sun wouldn't set for another hour, so there was plenty of space on the lawn. "How about over here?" Mia led the way to a grassy spot between two big trees and helped Mom spread out the blankets.

"Hey!" Clover called as she walked her bike over.

"Perfect timing," Mom said. "We just got here." She and Gram introduced themselves to Clover's moms, Alessandra and Jess, while Clover and Mia tore into a bag of potato chips. Mia brought Clover up to date on the fruit-fly situation.

"That Potsworth guy is the worst!" Clover said. "We've got to nail him on this. Can we go out there tomorrow?"

"Everything's closed until Monday," Mia said. "But yeah . . . we need to do something."

Half an hour went by before Dad found them. "I had to park in another county," he said, looking around at the growing crowd. "And now I'm famished from my journey." He passed out sandwiches, sodas, and his famous Fourth of July pyrotechnic brownies, and everyone dug in.

When they were finished, Mia and Clover went to the playground before it got dark. Mia's Boston friends would have thought that was too elementary-schoolish. She loved that Clover didn't care about stuff like that.

The swings were full of little kids, so Mia and Clover took a few lazy twirls on the merry-go-round thing while they waited. As Mia spun around, she saw a sign she'd never noticed when she lived here before.

"No adults allowed except in the company of a child?" she read. "That's weird."

"Not really," Clover said. Two swings had opened up, so they walked over. "There are creepers all over the place."

"What do you mean?" Mia asked, but her stomach twisted as she climbed on her swing. She was pretty sure she knew.

"Just . . . jerks," Clover said. She pumped her legs, and Mia did, too, until they were swinging side by side, as high as they could. "When we were visiting my grandmother in

Florida last year, I was walking on the beach. Just by myself because it was all cloudy and nobody else wanted to go out. And I walked farther than I was supposed to because I like picking up shells." She looked at Mia, who nodded. Shells were her favorite thing about the beach, too.

"I finally turned around when it started to rain a little," Clover said, sailing into the sky. "And that's when I noticed there was nobody else on the beach. Except one guy walking toward me."

Mia's heart sped up, and her arms felt all shaky. She would have jumped off the swing if Clover hadn't been in the middle of her story.

"When we were maybe fifty yards apart, the guy pulled his baggy swim trunks way off to the side, so everybody could see what was under there. So *I* could see."

"That's so gross!" Mia said. "What did you do?"

"It's not like I could turn around. The rain was picking up, and I had to get back." Clover stopped pumping and slowed down. Mia did, too, until they were just swaying a little. The setting sun had turned all peach-pink and was just brushing the peaks of the Adirondack Mountains on the other side of the lake.

"So I just kept going." Clover swallowed hard. "I got closer and closer, and he kept holding his shorts like that. I wanted to run, but I'd have to run right past him, and what if he grabbed me or something?"

"Clover, that's so awful." Mia reached out and put a hand on her shoulder. "I would have been terrified."

"I was." Clover took a deep breath and let it out. "But then I figured that's exactly what that jerk wanted. To scare me. He was doing that messed-up thing with his swimsuit because he *wanted* me to be afraid. And I just . . . I don't know. I felt like I had to pretend I wasn't. Like maybe if he thought I wasn't scared, everything would be all right."

Mia stared at her. "So what'd you do?"

"When I was about to pass him, I looked right at his face. He was looking away then, at the ocean, but I stared him in the face and said, 'Hello!' in this really loud voice."

"Clover! Seriously?" Mia couldn't imagine doing that. She probably would have turned around and kept running in the wrong direction forever. "What did he do?"

"He kind of freaked out," Clover said. "He jumped and dropped his handful of shorts and did this quick nod. And then he walked away really fast." Clover bit her lip. "I kept checking to make sure he didn't turn around, and then when he didn't and I was a ways down the beach, I ran home and told my moms what happened."

Mia actually couldn't imagine doing that, either. Her parents would flip if she'd wandered off on a deserted beach like that. "Did you get in trouble for walking so far?"

"Not really," Clover said. "They were glad I said something, and they called the police. But we went home the next day, so I don't know if they ever caught him."

"Wow." Mia watched as the sun sank into the mountains. "Bet you never walked on the beach again after that."

"No, I still do when we visit." Clover squinted at the sun. "It feels different, though. Like . . . I don't know. Like a shirt you used to love that has an ugly stain on it that won't come out. But I'm not gonna let some creep take the beach away."

"Yeah." Mia thought about that as the sun disappeared and realized how much she'd lost this past year since her accident. She used to love the feel of the balance beam under her bare feet. And she'd missed her gymnastics friends so much when she stopped hanging out with them. It wasn't even fun to watch competitions on TV with her mom anymore. They used to love that. But it seemed too late to get any of those things back.

"We should go." Mia stood up from her swing. "The fireworks will start soon."

By the time they got back to the blanket, an Eagles tribute band was playing in the waterfront tent, and the adults were singing along to "Hotel California." Clover's moms were really good singers but didn't seem to mind that no one else was.

"Mia! I've been waiting for you to get back." Gram held up what looked like an empty jar. But then something glowed inside it.

"You found a firefly!" Mia hadn't seen a single one since they got back to Vermont, but Gram always seemed to find them.

"Do you know how bioluminescence works?" Gram said, turning the jar.

Mia did, but she said, "How?" And that made Gram light up, too.

"It's a chemical reaction inside the firefly's body," Gram said. "The fireflies control when they flash, and they do it for a bunch of reasons. Most related to finding a mate. The males are always showing off, lighting up. And then females of the same species answer." She let her firefly go free, and it flashed off into the trees.

"What if the female firefly isn't into the male who's calling her?" Clover asked.

"Well . . ." Gram's eyes practically glowed at that question. "There's actually one species of firefly where the female signals to males of a different species. Males they don't have any interest in mating with."

"So what do they do if those other males show up?" Mia asked.

"Eat them," Gram said.

All the moms applauded at that.

"Ouch," Dad said. "Speaking of light, who needs a sparkler?"

Everyone did, so he passed around the box and held a lighter until they were all lit. Mia and Clover stood up with their sparklers, kicked off their flip-flops, and twirled around, making swirling trails of light. It was like the swings. With her Boston friends, Mia would have felt too old to dance with sparklers, but with Clover, it was just fun.

"Spell out your name!" Clover looped her sparkler to make a fancy cursive C.

"Mine's easy!" Mia sparkled out her three letters.

"Oh! We used to do this when I was a kid." Jess jumped up and spelled out her name, too.

Alessandra tried to join in but only made it to the D before her sparkler faded. "I don't think I like this game! It's not fair to people with long names," she said, and everyone laughed.

"Hey, the real fireworks are starting!" Dad called.

"Sticks in here!" Mom held up a cup of water she had waiting so nobody would step on the hot ends. Everyone fizzled their sparklers cool and settled in to watch as red and blue fountains of fire exploded over the bay.

Mia loved listening to the waves as the fireworks lit up

the lake. She loved that they were watching with Gram this year, that she'd found that first firefly of the summer and gotten to tell Mia and Clover about making light. And Mia especially loved that she had a new friend. One who was brave enough for both of them.

CHAPTER 11

The Cricket-Bot Plan

Gram called Saturday morning and said the fruit-fly situation was much better. It didn't seem like any more had hatched, and Mia was happy to hear that. But it reminded her that she had cricket work to do, too.

Clover came over to work on the Chirp Challenge banner for next weekend. Mia practiced her pitch for the farmers market and the restaurants they planned to visit afterward. Before Clover left, Mia told her what Daniel had said about everything taking too long, like the harvesting.

"Are you sure we trust that guy?" Clover asked.

Mia hesitated. "Not really?" She still thought there was a chance Daniel might be working with Mr. Potsworth somehow. "But either way, the harvest thing is an issue.

I was watching him. And maybe this is dumb, but I started thinking about Anna's robot. You know how it can pick things up and swivel and everything?"

"That's not dumb. It's brilliant!" Clover said, rolling up the banner. "Everything's automated these days, and if Daniel does leave, your grandmother will need quicker ways to do stuff. I bet Anna will totally be on board for this."

Clover was right. On Monday morning, they found Anna at camp. She still had red-white-and-blue-striped nails from the holiday weekend and was trying to make her robot pick up a gummy bear. "I'm trying to program it to feed me snacks while I watch TV."

"We have a proposal for your robot if you're interested," Clover said.

"Could you program it to shake something?" Mia asked as the robot claw crushed a yellow gummy bear.

"Sure. What for?"

"To shake crickets into bins." Mia went on to explain her idea. If Daniel or whoever replaced him got the bins set up, Anna could program the robot arm to shake crickets off the condos. They could put it on a timer—you could do that with robots, right?—and set it up so the robot would repeat the cycle four or five times, and then a buzzer would go off when it was done. That way, a worker could get it started but then leave to do other jobs while the robot handled the harvest.

Anna was nodding slowly the whole time Mia talked. "Sure. I think that's possible."

"Really?" Mia was afraid to hope. "So . . . is there any chance you'd want to work with us?"

"That'd be great," Anna said. "Want to come over after camp to brainstorm?"

"Sure!" Clover answered for both of them, so Mia texted her mom, and they rode their bikes to Anna's house after camp. It was up on the hill near the University of Vermont. Both Anna's parents worked there; her mom taught computer science, and her dad was in charge of something in the admissions office.

"You ride up this hill every day?" Clover asked, lifting her shirt to wipe sweat from her face at a stoplight.

Anna nodded. "Mom refuses to drive me. She says if I'm going to spend all my time making stuff in the basement instead of exercising, I should at least get to camp on my own power."

"It could be worse," Mia said. "Our moms made us do this Warrior Camp thing."

"It's not *that* bad," Clover said as they pulled into Anna's driveway.

"What's Warrior Camp?" Anna asked.

"A place where totally ripped coaches torture weak, unsuspecting kids," Mia said, and stood up to pedal. At least she was getting in shape again, though. Without

Warrior Camp, she might not have made it up this miserable hill.

When they got to Anna's house, her parents were at work, but her older sister, Prima, was at the kitchen table, surrounded by books and papers full of diagrams. The scent that filled the kitchen made Mia's stomach grumble—a mix of onions, oil, and spices. "What's that amazing smell?"

"Pakora?" Anna looked at her sister.

Prima nodded and pointed to a plate of fried vegetable fritters on the counter. "Mom made them before she left, and I've already eaten a whole plateful, so go for it."

Anna took the plate and some paper towels, and they headed down to the basement.

It was nothing like Mia's basement, where there were just moving boxes and laundry. This was a workshop with even more tools and supplies than the maker space at school.

"This is amazing!" Clover said.

"It's pretty great to have," Anna said. "Prima's in school at MIT, so she hogs it up with projects when she's home for the summer, but the rest of the year, it's pretty much mine. Here . . ." She put the plate of pakoras down on the counter and grabbed a pencil and a big piece of paper. "Let's talk about your harvesting robot while we eat." She started sketching. "It'll have to be a six-axis robot like this one, with articulated arms and something that can grip the cardboard because it's not very thick, right?"

"Right," Mia said through a mouthful of pakora. She didn't know what an articulated arm was, but she was grateful that Anna did.

For another half hour, Anna drew and asked questions, and Clover and Mia did their best to answer. By then, the pakoras were gone, and the basement was feeling stuffy, so they went outside, and Anna led them to a wooden fort tucked back in the trees.

"Prima and I built this before she left for college." Anna pulled down a rope ladder, and they all climbed up.

"It's really cool." Mia liked how sturdy it felt. Her old friend Lily had a tree fort, but Lily's dad hadn't been much of a builder, so half the time, her fort felt like it might blow over.

"Hey . . . thanks for asking me to work on your project," Anna said.

"Oh my gosh, thank *you*," Mia said. "There's no way we could do this part ourselves."

Anna nodded. "It's kind of a perfect job for me. And I really do like working on teams. It's just . . ." She looked at Clover.

"Yeah. Eli's kind of a pain."

"I told my mom about it, and she was so mad, I was

afraid she was going to march in there and grab him by the collar or something. I figured it would be easier to just work by myself. Before Mom taught at UVM and met Dad, she worked at a tech company out in Silicon Valley, and there were, like, four women in the whole place. She'd never told me this before—it only came up when I told her about Eli—but she got harassed a lot. She was the only woman there who wasn't white—she's Indian, in case you didn't figure that out—and she says cute white guys like Eli were the worst because they thought they were God's gift to the world and just assumed she'd want to go out with them." Anna took a deep breath and looked up. "I don't know why I'm telling you all this, but I just . . ."

"No, I get it," Mia said. She did. And now she was extra glad they'd asked Anna for help. "I'm just happy you want to work with us. And I hope we can hang out more, too."

"Hey!" Anna stood up. "You should show me some of your warrior course stuff. Didn't you say it was like a jungle gym situation? Look . . ." She pointed out the fort's back window, where monkey bars led to another rope ladder.

"Maybe Clover can show you something," Mia said. "All I can do is hang."

"You're getting better at it, though!" Clover said, laughing. "Weren't you up to, like, fifteen seconds last week?"

"I want to try!" Anna said, so they took turns hanging from the bar and timing one another. Mia made it sixteen seconds before she dropped into the pine needles below. Clover did forty-five seconds. Anna made it to twelve, and then they all climbed up and did it again.

"Let's try all at once!" Clover said. So on the count of three, they jumped up from the ground and grabbed the bars.

"My arms already feel like they're going to fall off!" Anna said after a few seconds. "You should have told me this gets harder every time!"

"You need to distract yourself," Clover said. "Think about robots or something."

"We need music," said Mia. When she and Eunice had to hold planks forever at gymnastics, they'd tap their feet out to the beat of some Renegade Kickboxers song, and that helped pass the time. But their phones were in the tree fort. "Somebody sing something!"

"Twinkle twinkle little star . . . ," Clover started. "My arms are falling off, yes they are . . ."

"That's not helping!" Anna started laughing so hard that she dropped, but Mia kept holding on.

"Sing something *better*!" she said. "I need quality music to get through this."

"One short day, in the Emerald City . . . ," Clover sang.

"Oh my gosh, I loved that show!" Anna said.

Mia's hands were slipping, but she managed to grunt out, "Me too!" before she dropped to the ground, and then Clover jumped down, too. It turned out all their grandmothers had taken them to see that Broadway musical, *Wicked*, that Clover's song was from.

"My favorite part was where Elphaba flew over the audience," Mia said.

"Right?" Anna's eyes were huge. "I kept trying to figure out how that pulley system worked so the whole thing was so smooth."

"Anna's going to be a Broadway special-effects engineer someday," Clover said as they headed back to the house for water.

"Maybe," Anna said. "But first, we have a cricket-harvesting robot to build."

The girls spent Tuesday morning at Launch Camp talking more about the robot. Mia and Clover made new plans to snoop on Mr. Potsworth, too, but that didn't exactly work out. After camp, they rode their bikes over to the food-processing plant, only to find that it was shut down for the whole week because of the holiday.

"That's okay," Clover said. "If he's out of town, he can't do any damage, and we have other things to focus on until he gets back."

They spent the rest of the week getting robot updates from Anna, preparing for the farmers market, practicing their pitches to local businesses, and surviving Warrior Camp. Clover was getting pretty good at the quad steps, and she made it to the ten-foot mark on the warped wall.

Mia wanted nothing to do with that wall, and even though her scraped-up shin was scabbed over now, she didn't like the quad steps, either. But on Thursday, she did manage to jump on the trampoline and stick her hands and feet on the spider wall a few times.

That little trampoline reminded Mia of the vault at her old gym. She used to love the vault. During the break at camp that day, she stopped to look in the gymnastics window to see if anybody was vaulting, but there were only kids on the bars and beam. The girl on the beam was really good, like Mia used to be. Mia rose on her toes, just a little, as she watched the girl lift and pivot. Then the Jamie lady came out the door. Mia's heels hit the floor.

"It's good to see you again!" Jamie said. "Don't forget, if you ever want to try a session with us, just let me know."

Mia shook her head and backed away. "I was just watching. I'm super busy."

She was busy. She'd almost finished her business plan at Launch Camp. She'd been helping with the crickets all week and taking Syd for walks to bark at strangers. She'd even been to a few of the extra Warrior Camp sessions they held in the evenings. She was up to thirty whole seconds of hanging from her bar now.

"You're going to be able to do the rings soon," Clover said as they walked out of camp on Thursday.

"Doubt it," Mia said. But she did feel a little stronger. She was even getting calluses on her palms, like weightlifters do.

"Hey!" a man's voice shouted. Mia's heart jumped into her throat, but it was only Mr. Jacobson. He jogged down the hall toward them, hugging a moose. It was wearing a pink headband and leotard. "I've been wanting to give you this," he said, handing it to Mia. "It's a sporty gymnast moose."

The moose was fat and lopsided, with enormous antlers. It looked like it would be about as elegant as Mia had been the last time she was on a balance beam. It would have been rude to remind Mr. Jacobson that she wasn't a gymnast now, so she just said thanks.

"And look!" He squeezed the moose's ear.

"Hello from Vermont!" it said.

"Wow." It wasn't just a sporty moose. It was a *talking* sporty moose. "Thanks."

"I know it's tough to move to a new town, so I thought you might like a buddy." Mr. Jacobson looked at Clover then. "Not that you don't already have buddies!"

They all laughed, and Mia and Clover went out to their

bikes. Mia shoved the moose into her gym bag, but its antlers wouldn't fit.

"That is a sad excuse for a moose," Clover said.

"I know. But he was trying to be nice. And he's helped Gram a bunch, so . . ." Mia shrugged and jumped on her bike. She could pretend to like the moose.

"All set for Saturday?" Clover asked as they started toward home.

"Sure," Mia said, even though she didn't feel ready. She figured that if she kept pretending to be brave, she might trick herself into feeling that way. Besides, everyone else was working so hard to help Gram keep her farm. Daniel was putting in extra hours. Anna had already figured out a new robot grip that could hold on to thin cardboard. Clover's Chirp Challenge banner looked amazing. And Mia had practiced her pitch so much she could do it in her sleep.

The thought of talking to all those people at the farmers market still made Mia's stomach feel floppy. But that was fine. She could talk crickets with a floppy stomach. She had to do whatever she could to keep Gram's farm going. She had to help Gram show Daniel and her parents and everyone that it wasn't time to give up. Mia took one hand off her handlebars and ran her thumb over the calluses on her palm. She was a warrior. She could do this. Right?

CHAPTER 12

The Chirp Challenge

On Saturday morning, Mom dropped off Mia and Clover at the farmers market. Mia had told her parents they wanted to spend the afternoon on Church Street after the market wrapped up. They said that was fine, and the girls could walk home when they were done. Mia didn't mention they'd be making business pitches instead of shopping for socks and eating ice cream. She didn't even tell Gram or Daniel or anybody else from Launch Camp. If nobody knew what you were planning, they couldn't laugh when it failed.

"Morning, ladies!" Daniel waved from the booth. He'd already spread out a blue tablecloth and fliers about the nutritional and ecological benefits of eating insects. "I have to take off by noon, but I can stay with you for a while. Ready to sell some crickets?"

"Yep!" Mia said. She and Clover set up the cricket tasting. They lined up tiny paper cups for samples and shook a few roasted crickets into each one.

It was only nine o'clock, but the market was bustling. Farmers unloaded crates of kale and zucchini, the lemonade lady had her juicer set up, and the Himalayan restaurant had a batch of momos cooking. Mia could smell them as she helped Clover hang the Chirp Challenge banner. She'd been too nervous to eat breakfast, but now she was hungry.

"Is it too early for momos?" she asked.

"It's never too early for momos," Clover said. They bought a plate to share before the market officially opened at ten. The family who ran the momo place lived near Gram, so Mia had known them since she was little.

"Thanks, Mr. Dorjee!" she said, and headed back to the cricket booth with a mouth full of doughy, spicy dumpling goodness.

Shoppers started arriving a little before ten. Daniel had to run back to his car because he forgot his phone.

"Think he really has a game today? Or is he having another sneaky meeting?" Mia asked as Daniel walked away.

"I thought of that, too. There's a game." Clover held

up her phone. "I checked online." She nudged Mia and pointed to a family of tourists heading for the booth. "Look, customers!"

"Cricket samples?" the mom said. "Ha! If only we'd brought Franklin, our pet chameleon, on this trip . . ."

The dad laughed, but the kids looked interested, and Mia knew this was her chance. Her heart raced, and the momos churned in her stomach, but she took a deep breath and imagined herself pitching on *Deal with the Sharks.* "Actually, crickets are the new superfood for people, too." She gave her whole talk about protein and sustainability and wrapped up with, "Would you like to sample some? We have sea salt and garlic, barbecue, and maple-flavored today."

"I want barbecue!" the littlest kid said.

Mia looked at the parents. "Is it okay if she tries them? She's not allergic to shellfish or anything, right?" They had a sign up at the booth warning people about that, but Mia still figured she shouldn't hand out crickets to kids unless their parents said it was okay.

"Better you than me," the dad said. "Go for it."

Mia handed the girl a little cup of crickets, and she poured them all into her mouth at once. "They're good!"

"Can I try some, too?" her older brother asked. Pretty soon, all the kids and the mom were chomping down on barbecue crickets.

Clover held a cup out to the dad. "Would you like to try one? No pressure, but I don't want you to feel left out."

"Do it, Daddy!" the little girl shouted. "They're crunchy!"

The dad made a face at the crickets, but then he nodded. "Actually, can I try maple? We are in Vermont, after all."

Mia gave him the sample, and he picked up a single cricket between two fingers. He tipped his head back, held it over his mouth, and made a face at the kids.

"You have to eat it, Daddy!" the little one shouted, and his whole family started chanting, "Eat it! Eat it!" They were so loud that a crowd gathered, and then the dad hammed it up even more.

His dramatic pose reminded Mia of Eli, mugging to have his picture taken, and that reminded her about the Chirp Challenge. "Hold on!" she said, just when it looked like the dad might stop goofing around and eat his cricket. "Before you do that, you should snap a photo with our banner. You're taking the Chirp Challenge, after all!"

The dad loved that. He took a picture, and then the whole family got more crickets and posed under the banner for a photo together. "Well, this will make for an interesting Christmas card," the mom said.

"Do you want to take some home to share with your friends?" Clover asked, shaking a five-dollar tub of barbecue crickets.

"Can we, Mom?" the girl asked.

"Sure." She dug into her purse, and by the time they left with three tubs of crickets—one of each flavor—a line had formed. It was even longer than Mr. Dorjee's momo line. Daniel raised his eyebrows and gave them a thumbs-up as he returned. "That banner is brilliant," he said, and jumped in to help with all the people who wanted to take cricket selfies.

Anna came by with her family, and they all took pictures, too.

"It's so nice to meet you," her dad said as he paid for a tub of barbecue crickets. "Anna told me her new friend had an interesting project, and I had to see this to believe it."

Mia couldn't help smiling. She loved that Anna already called her a friend. "Well, Anna's harvesting robot is a key part of our business plan."

Anna's mom nodded. "We got to see the plans last night."

"Prima helped me figure out a few things." Anna nodded toward her sister, who had a mouthful of chocolate croissant. "I just need a couple more parts, but I should be able to run a demo soon." She looked over her shoulder at the growing line. "We'd better let you go. You have fans waiting!"

Mia and Clover waved goodbye and got back to work. People were having so much fun with the Chirp Challenge that Mia forgot how nervous she'd been and laughed along with them. Sometimes she came out from the booth and took pictures so groups of people could all be in the photo, eating crickets together. One lady who'd come on her bicycle asked Mia to do that, too. She wanted her bike in the shot.

"There you go!" Mia said, handing her phone back to her, along with a business card that had the farm's website. "Have a great day!"

Clover grabbed her arm when she stepped back in the booth. "Mia! Do you know who that was?"

Mia shook her head.

"That was Jackie Obasanjo!" When Mia didn't react, Clover added, "The mayor! You just took a Chirp Challenge photo of the *mayor*!"

"Oh wow!" Mia stood on her tiptoes so she could see Mayor Obasanjo walking her bike away through the market crowd. "I didn't know. Brett Cunningham was the mayor when we lived here before."

"Yeah. Ms. Obasanjo ran against him and won. She's super cool. I follow her . . . hold on . . ." Clover poked at her phone. Then she gasped. "Mia, look!"

Mia took the phone. "Whoa!" The mayor had just posted the photo Mia took for her with the caption: *Great day at the Burlington farmers market! Got to sample some amazing BBQ crickets from innovative local entrepreneurs.*

Check them out when you get a chance! #ChirpChallenge
#MadeInVermont

"She linked to Gram's website!" Mia said.

Clover grabbed her phone back. "She has sixty thousand followers! This is amazing!"

"Hey!" Daniel shouted. "Are you going to help me with this line or what?"

Mia and Clover put away the phone and got back to the line. For the next three hours, they filled sample cups, took Chirp Challenge photos, shared Gram's brochures, and sold crickets. Daniel had to take off at noon but promised James would swing by before the game to pick up the banner and money and everything when the market ended.

By the time he showed up at two, Mia and Clover had one tub of sea salt and garlic crickets left for sale. Mr. Dorjee came over and bought it while they were packing up.

"Well, that was a success," Clover said as she rolled up the banner. "Ready for the second part of today's mission?"

"Yep!" Mia said. "Let's hit Church Street!"

It was funny, she thought as she folded the blue tablecloth and loaded it into James's truck. Five hours ago, she'd had a stomachache just thinking about walking into restaurants to talk about crickets. Now it didn't seem like a big deal at all. Maybe some of Clover's attitude really was rubbing off on her. And after all, if the cool new mayor loved their crickets, who could possibly say no?

CHAPTER 13

Pitching Crickets

Convincing businesspeople to serve crickets to their customers was harder than getting people to eat one for a selfie, it turned out. For starters, half the businesspeople weren't there.

"You'll have to talk to Tony on Monday," said the guy at the sports bar.

"Christina won't be in until tomorrow," said the hostess at the Mexican restaurant. Two other managers were too busy to talk, and Roy from Anderson's Pub was out having knee surgery.

"I don't see why the world has to come to a stop because of Roy's knee," Clover said as they collapsed on a bench outside the pub. Mia was frustrated, too. Her pitch was ready, but she never got past, "Hello, I'm Mia Barnes with Green Mountain Cricket Farm, and I'd like to talk with you about an exciting opportunity . . ."

They bought lemonade from the cart outside the candle store. Mia looked at the cinnamon-scented candles in the window while she sipped hers. Could you put crickets in a candle? She didn't know why anyone would want to, but things were feeling desperate. "What's left on our list?" she asked Clover.

"Tom and Harry's Ice Cream, Mazzella's Pizza, Giordano's Italian Restaurant, that French place, and the Chocolate Shoppe."

"Let's try that one next," Mia said. The manager would probably be out having elbow surgery or something, but at least they could get salted caramels.

The shop was quiet when Mia and Clover walked in, probably because everybody was in line for Tom and Harry's Ice Cream across the street. There was a family sampling peanut butter cups with a worker at the counter, and another lady stood at the register. Mia walked up to her.

"Hi, I'm Mia Barnes with Green Mountain Cricket Farm, and I'd like to talk with you about an exciting opportunity for your store." Mia paused and waited to hear where the chocolate store owner might be today. Maybe France, sampling new chocolates, she decided.

But the lady at the counter smiled and said, "Sure, go

for it! I'm Caroline, and I'm the owner here. I'm always looking for fresh ideas."

Mia was so surprised that she stared for a few seconds until Clover nudged her. "We think your customers would love the novelty of a cricket chocolate treat," Mia said, and pulled out one of Gram's handouts. She gave Caroline her whole pitch, just the way she'd practiced. "I can give you samples if you'd like to experiment with a recipe or two." Mia held out one of the sample bags she and Clover had prepared. "We have different flavors, but plain roasted crickets would probably be best with chocolate."

"Hmm." The chocolate lady opened the sample bag and ate a couple. She was different from the people at the market. She chewed thoughtfully, nodded, and then looked at her fancy chocolates behind the glass. "Any idea if other chocolate makers have tried this?" she asked. "I wonder if it would be best as a topping—like a cricket on top of a truffle—or something else."

"That's an interesting question," Mia said. She had a tote bag full of articles about fancy restaurants serving crickets in sauces, but she'd never heard of anybody except Gram putting crickets on chocolate or in chocolate or any-where near chocolate. "A cricket-topped truffle sounds good."

"Or you know what?" Clover jumped in. "You have that chocolate with the rice crisps, right? The crunchy one?"

Caroline nodded. "That's one of our best sellers."

"You could swap the rice crisps out for crickets!"

"And call them cricket crispies!" Mia added.

"I like that idea!" Caroline looked down at the sample pack in her hands. "We'll try a small batch with these and see how it goes. Where can I buy more if it works out?"

"You can order online." Mia gave her a business card with the website. "Thanks so much for talking with us!"

Mia was so excited she forgot all about getting salted caramels. She grabbed Clover's arm when they got outside. "Can you imagine how amazing it'll be if they're selling chocolate crispies with Gram's crickets on Church Street?"

"We need to follow up with her," Clover said, and Mia made a note to do that in a few weeks.

From there, they went to Mazzella's, where the owner's son thought cricket pizza was a fun idea but said he'd have to check with his dad. Mia and Clover lucked out at Tom and Harry's Ice Cream, though. The owners had just been brainstorming seasonal flavors for Halloween.

"This is perfect!" Harry said. "We'll do a vanilla base with toffee crunch, coconut, and chocolate-covered crickets. We can call it Creepy Coconut Cricket Crunch!"

Mia and Clover gave him a sample bag and business card and then ordered ice-cream cones. Mia got rainbow sherbet, and Clover got chocolate coffee swirl.

By the time they finished and walked home, Mia's dad

was putting on water for spaghetti. "Anybody know where the salt is?" he asked.

"Check behind the moose," Mia said.

"Say what?" Mom looked around until she spotted the sporty moose on the counter, over in the corner. "Why has this moose taken up residence in front of my spice rack?"

"Sorry—I left it there when I got home the other day." The truth was, Mia didn't want that moose in its gymnastics leotard in her room, reminding her about what she couldn't do anymore. Reminding her of other stuff, too.

"Did you hear from Gram today?" Mia asked.

"Yep," Dad said. "Stopped by on our way home, and she says the fruit flies are under control. She's thankful it wasn't some other insect that carries cricket diseases."

"There are cricket diseases?" Mia asked.

"Apparently. She was telling me about this virus called . . . what was it?" he asked Mom.

"CPV."

"Right. Cricket paralysis virus. I guess it's wiped out entire farms before. Gram says if that ever got in the warehouse, she'd be finished."

"Couldn't she just start over with new crickets?" Mia asked.

"No," Dad said. "Grab me the colander, would you?" He dumped in the spaghetti, and steam rose around his face. "That virus apparently gets into everything. She says a farm in Quebec just had it wipe out their whole population. They cleaned everything out and brought in new eggs, but as soon as those crickets hatched, they got it, too."

"Wow," Mia said. "But fruit flies don't carry it, right?"

"Actually, they can," Dad said, "but Gram's convinced those flies came from a lab, so they'd be clean. Nobody could raise that many on a bunch of old bananas in their kitchen."

When Dad went to find some cheese, Clover turned to Mia and whispered, "Unless you have a really big kitchen." Her eyes were huge, and Mia understood why. Was Mr. Potsworth raising fruit flies at his food-processing plant?

Mia nodded. They'd keep that in mind when they went out there next week. For now, at least, Gram's crickets were safe.

"It's wild how much can go wrong with a cricket farm," Clover said, ladling sauce on her spaghetti.

"Yup." Mia sprinkled cheese on hers and dug in. She wondered how the pasta would taste made with cricket protein. And that reminded her of their afternoon on Church Street and their morning of Chirp Challenge selfies.

Mia looked over at Clover and smiled. "But sometimes things go right, too."

CHAPTER 14

Spies in Pink High-Tops

On Monday afternoon, Mia and Clover rode their bikes out to Mr. Potsworth's food-processing plant. "To case the place," Clover explained. "We need to scope it out from the outside before we break in so—"

"Before we *break in*?" Mia stopped her bike and stared at Clover.

"Relax." Clover pushed her bike behind a hedge outside the food-processing plant and motioned for Mia to join her among the bushes. "We're not *really* breaking in. In this book I read, this girl named Paloma and her friends had to get into a museum after hours, and she didn't want to break in, either," Clover said.

"Good." Mia felt grateful for Paloma's common sense. If Paloma-in-the-story had busted in through a window, there was no telling what Clover might have Mia signed up for.

"So they wait until everybody's leaving for the night and unlock a back door," Clover said. "They come back later, and there's no breaking in necessary."

"And that's what you want to do here? Today?"

"No, tomorrow. Today we just need to learn what time this place empties out." Clover untied her jacket from her waist and made a little nest for them on the ground, where they could peek through the bushes at the building's back door. "It's four fifty," she said, pulling a tiny pair of binoculars from her backpack. "I'm guessing their work day ends at five."

Sure enough, a few minutes later, the back door opened, and two workers came out.

"This is good," Clover whispered, lowering her binoculars.

"What's good?"

"That door closes by itself. But it's slow, probably because they don't want it closing on workers who are carrying stuff. That'll give us plenty of time to stick a rock or something in the door as it's closing, to keep it from latching. And then— Shh! Here come more."

Mia watched as more people streamed out the door and headed for their cars.

"Seven . . . eight . . . nine . . . ," Clover whisper-counted. "And look at the other door! It's him!" she hissed as Chet Potsworth came out the front. They'd seen his picture on the company website, and it was definitely him. He drove away in a shiny red convertible.

"There should be one more. They have ten employees." Clover had learned that on the website, too. Sure enough, a tall bald guy came out and drove off in the last car. Clover looked at her phone. "It's only five after five. We'll have plenty of time to do what we need to do."

"Which is . . . what again?" Mia asked as they got on their bikes and started for home.

"Search for evidence," Clover said. "I'm telling you, bad guys in mysteries always get careless. That Potsworth guy's going to wish he never dared to mess with your gram's farm."

Clover sounded like some gritty tough-guy detective from one of her mysteries. Mia wished she felt that confident, but she was pretty sure the real world didn't follow mystery-novel rules.

Still, she rode back to the processing plant with Clover after Warrior Camp the next day. They got their bikes tucked away in the bushes and settled in to wait.

"Look!" Clover whispered. "He's leaving early." It was only four thirty when Mr. Potsworth came out the door.

"Have a great night now!" he boomed to someone still inside. Then he got in his car and drove away.

"Wonder where he's going," Clover said.

"Gram's still at the farm, and so is Daniel," Mia said. "He wouldn't try anything now."

The other workers didn't stick around long. After the ninth person left, Clover said, "Okay. That car must belong to the last worker." She pointed to a green Subaru around a corner from the back door. "This is perfect. As soon as they come out, they'll turn to go to their car, and then I can run in and jam the door." She picked up a good-size wood chip. "This should do it." She crept to the edge of the bushes and crouched in a runner's pose, staring at the building.

Five o'clock came. Then 5:05 . . . and then 5:10. The door stayed closed.

Mia shifted and sat up on her knees. Her right foot had fallen asleep. "Clover, maybe—"

"Shh!" Just then, the door opened, and a man came out, holding a phone to his ear. The second he turned the corner, Clover took off running.

Mia's breath caught in her throat. Her heart thudded so hard she was afraid the guy heading for his car would hear it and turn around.

But Clover was already out of his sight, tiptoe-running toward the slowly closing door. It was all the way down the building, though. Mia wasn't sure Clover was going to make it.

Just before the door closed, she put on a superhuman burst of speed, grabbed the handle, and stuck her wood chip between the door and frame. Then she ran, quick as a cat, along the building and tumbled into the bushes beside Mia as the guy's car started up.

"That was impressive," Mia said. She was the one breathing hard, even though Clover had done all the running.

Clover grinned, and they watched the Subaru drive away. They waited a few minutes to make sure it was quiet, and then Clover said, "Let's go."

They ran to the door. Clover held it and motioned Mia to hurry, so she darted inside. As soon as she did, bright lights came on.

Mia froze.

Clover did, too. Then she pointed to a light fixture on the wall. "It's okay," she whispered. "They're just motion activated. This will actually help us out."

Mia followed Clover down a long, gleaming counter that ran through the center of the room. The whole place was made of stainless steel. Counters and ovens and automated assembly-line stuff.

Too bad Mr. Potsworth isn't on Gram's side, Mia

thought. *He'd have her cricket-harvesting problem solved in no time.*

"This way." Clover walked down an aisle. Pipes of all sizes crisscrossed above them. Along the far wall, there were six enormous steel tanks of something.

A fan hummed to life overhead and scared Mia so much she thought she might pass out. Clover kept prowling up and down the counters and rows of machinery. "Do you see anything that looks weird?"

"Everything looks weird."

"I mean clues."

"Nope." All Mia saw was a whole lot of shiny food-processing equipment. All she felt was her heart racing out of control, her breath catching in her throat, and her post-camp Gatorade churning in her stomach. "Clover, I'm freaking out. We shouldn't be here."

"We didn't break in," Clover reminded her.

"We're *trespassing.*"

"We'll go soon. Let's just finish this lap. See if anything looks like a fruit-fly nursery."

"Do you really think he'd raise them in the same place he's packaging baked goods?" Mia asked.

"Do you really think a person who's rotten enough to sabotage your gram's farm would worry about selling people buggy maple muffins?"

She had a good point. "Okay, but—" Something

thumped, and Mia stopped walking. "Was that a car door?"

"What?" Clover stopped, too. A door slammed in the front of the building. Then footsteps.

Mia sucked in her breath and looked at Clover. Should they run for the back door? If whoever was here came into the big processing room, they'd see them for sure.

"Here!" Clover grabbed Mia's hand and yanked her behind those big steel tanks along the wall, just as another door opened and closed.

"Anybody here?" a booming voice called from the other side of the tall freezers. It was Mr. Potsworth, Mia was sure.

She held her breath.

More footsteps.

Kathunk . . . Kathunk . . . Kathunk . . .

Clover elbowed Mia, then pointed frantically at their feet.

Mia looked down, and her heart trampolined into her throat. The steel tanks they were hiding behind were elevated, so there was about a foot of space between them and the floor. If Mr. Potsworth was looking, he'd see their shoes. And Mia wasn't wearing just any shoes. How could she have been so dumb? What kind of sleuth wore bright-pink high-tops on a spy mission?

Mia looked back at Clover in a panic. Clover put a

finger to her lips, then pointed to the pipes above their heads. She paused, and when Mr. Potsworth's footsteps grew faint again, she jumped up, grabbed one, and pulled her knees up, high enough so the tanks would hide them. She jerked her head for Mia to do the same.

There was no time to think. Mia hoisted herself up, too. She dangled there, swaying between the tanks and the wall as the footsteps approached again. Then Mr. Potsworth's phone rang.

"Hello?" he said. The footsteps were close. Then they stopped.

"No, I had to pop back in, and lights were on, so I came in to check . . .

"I know . . ."

Mia's arms started shaking.

"Yeah . . .

"Well, last time this happened, a squirrel had gotten in somehow, so . . .

"Ha! No, I don't think fruit flies would trigger the motion lights."

Mia heard Clover gasp. She was trying to process what Mr. Potsworth had said, but her hands were burning and sweating and making the bar slippery. Her arms felt as if they might pull right out of the sockets. How long was he going to stand there?

"Okay, then . . ."

Hang on, Mia thought. *Hang on.*

She could feel the calluses on her right hand ripping open. *Battle scars*, she told herself.

Hang on.

"Yeah, I don't see any problems here . . ."

She wasn't going to make it. Her hands were slipping. Her arms were on fire.

Hang on.

"Okay. See you soon . . ."

Footsteps. Loud ones, but then they faded away.

Not yet. Not yet.

The second Mia heard the door slam, she dropped to the ground.

Clover thumped down and grabbed her arm. "Let's get out of here," she whispered, creeping along the wall to the back door. She opened it a sliver—"His car's gone"—and motioned Mia out. They raced to their bikes and rode halfway home before Clover blurted out, "Mia, that was awful, and I'm so sorry. I went all supersleuth on you and just . . . sorry." A tear streaked down her cheek.

Mia's arms were still burning, and now she felt an angry heat growing in her chest, too. But it wasn't directed at Clover. "Did you hear what he said to whoever that was on the phone?"

Clover sniffed and nodded.

"He laughed about it!"

"I know," Clover said. She looked at Mia as they coasted onto their street. "You're not mad at me?"

"I'm mad at *him*." Mia parked her bike by the garage.

"At least we know for sure now," Clover said. "We should tell somebody. Right?"

Mia hesitated. "We can't do that without admitting we broke into the processing plant."

"We didn't really—" Clover began, but Mia held up her hand.

"We entered without permission." Mia sighed. "Now that we know, we'll just have to make sure he can't hurt the farm again. Maybe I'll talk with Gram about installing some cameras." Mia looked at Clover, still on her bike. "Can you stay for dinner?"

"Better not," she said, holding up her phone. "The moms are already mad because I didn't text after Warrior Camp. But I'll see you in the morning?"

"Definitely," Mia said, and headed inside.

The kitchen smelled like pot roast, and Mom was making a salad. "There you are!" she said. "We were getting ready to send out a search party!"

"We rode our bikes after camp." It wasn't a lie, but Mia felt the real truth poking at her insides. "Want me to set the table?"

"That would be great," Mom said. "Wash your hands first."

Mia sucked in her breath when the hot water hit her torn-up palms.

Mom looked over. "Whoa. They're not messing around with that Warrior Camp."

"Yeah," Mia said. "I was hanging on a bar for a long time today." That was true, at least.

The whole scene ran through Mia's head like an action movie. She still couldn't believe it. Mia Barnes and her friend had pulled off a secret spy mission. They'd found the truth about the fruit flies. They'd almost gotten caught, but thanks to Clover's quick thinking, they'd disappeared into the pipes.

And Mia had held on.

She'd held on.

Longer than she ever thought she could.

CHAPTER 15

Monster Donuts and Impossible Plans

A lot happened over the next three weeks. Mia talked with Gram about security cameras, but Gram said there was no way they could afford them. Not unless they found new investors, and even though she was still scheduling meetings, she seemed less hopeful. One day, Mia tried to buy some cricket powder so Aidan could try a new recipe for Cookies for a Cause, and Gram wouldn't let her pay for it. When Mia tried again, Gram let out a snort of a laugh and told her when you're $40,000 in debt, you don't worry about a twenty-dollar bag of cricket powder.

Mia had been hoping the businesses she and Clover visited would order more crickets. That wouldn't solve Gram's problems, but it might help. Mia made herself a note to follow up with the pizza place and Chocolate Shoppe. She didn't dread talking to business owners anymore and had actually come to enjoy making sales calls with Clover.

Mia would never admit it to Mom, but she was loving both of her camps, too. She liked the way her body felt after she pushed herself at Warrior Camp—sore and tired but also strong. She hadn't tried the warped wall or the rings yet, but she could almost get through the quad steps now, and she was getting better at the climbing wall.

Mia loved the chaos of Launch Camp, too—the way everybody showed up full of ideas and cheered one another on. She and Clover and Anna worked together almost every day now. Anna had them helping to solder wires for the cricket robot. Zoya called the girls her Three Entrepreneurial Musketeers.

"Team meeting!" Zoya called out on the Monday morning before the Vermont Launch Junior competition. "I have some updates before you get to work."

"Can't I listen from here?" Eli was already at his computer.

"Sure, if you don't want breakfast." Zoya opened a big green-and-white-striped box.

"You brought Vermonstrosities!" Eli slammed his laptop shut, raced to the table, and lifted an enormous coconut-sprinkled chocolate donut to his mouth.

"Whoa!" It was twice as big as any donut Mia had ever seen.

"Vermonstrosities is the new donut shop that opened on Cherry Street last year," Clover explained, picking out a maple-glazed donut the size of her face. "Their slogan is 'Donut be afraid.'"

"Ha!" Mia chose a custard cream donut, which must have been dusted with half a bag of confectioners' sugar, and settled in next to Clover with her notebook. She hoped Zoya's meeting would be fast. Mia wasn't scrambling to get ready for the competition like everyone else, but she had a lot to do. Gram's open house was only a week away, so she wanted to work on plans, and she also wanted to update her list of businesses to visit. Maybe Vermonstrosities would try a cricket donut. Mia opened her notebook while Zoya started talking.

"First, a calendar note. Tomorrow we'll be walking up to UVM to hear a talk from the owner of Five Dogs Apparel."

"What's his name, and what's he talking about?" Eli asked.

"*Her* name is Anne Marie Spangler," Zoya said, "and *she* is talking about her path to running a major apparel company that started right here in Vermont. It's part of a speaker series at the college."

Zoya looked down at her clipboard. "Next we need to

talk about Vermont Launch Junior. There's still time to sign up." She glanced at Mia when she said that. "But I definitely need permission slips by Thursday."

Mia went back to her notebook. There was no point in her doing the competition. Not when everybody else had been working on it for so long. She added *Visit Vermonstrosities—chocolate cricket donut?* to her to-do list.

But then Clover slid the permission slip in front of her face and tapped on the list of judging criteria. "Your cricket farm plan is actually a perfect fit for this. You should enter!"

Mia glanced at the guidelines. It did seem like she had a pretty good start. "But it's *this* Saturday! And you're already on a team. I wouldn't want to do it by myself."

"Hey, Zoya!" Clover called. "Can a person be on more than one team for the competition?"

"Sure," Zoya said. "I've had kids who wrote code for multiple projects, and they presented with all of them."

"Great!" Clover turned back to Mia, as if that settled it.

"I don't know . . ." Mia's stomach felt floppy, and not just because she'd scarfed down an entire Vermonstrosity. "I don't think we have enough to work with."

"I'll do it with you," Anna said. "We can include a robot arm demo. It'll be fun!"

"And it would be great exposure for the cricket farm,"

Clover said. "The newspaper sends photographers and everything. We can bring the banner, and the farm might even be on TV!"

Mia had to admit that sounded promising. Gram was having all those meetings with her maybe-investors, and it might help if they saw the farm featured on TV. What if Vermont Launch Junior could really make a difference? What if they won? That wasn't likely, and fifty dollars and a trophy wouldn't solve Gram's problems, but a mentor might help. Even if they didn't win, more people would hear about the farm.

"Okay," Mia said.

"Really?" Clover looked surprised.

"Yay!" Anna cheered and high-fived them both. "We are going to rock this thing. Here's to the Three Entrepreneurial Musketeers!"

Mia had her mom sign her permission slip that night, before she filled in any of the project details on the paperwork. She wasn't ready to share her plans yet. And that turned out to be fine, because Mom was busy on the phone when Mia slid the paper in front of her.

"Yes, things are evolving," Mom said as she signed. "She may be more open to the idea."

Mia started to go upstairs, but then she heard Mom say, "If you draw up an offer, I'll make sure she gives it real consideration."

"Who was that?" Mia said when Mom hung up.

"I've been on the phone half the afternoon," Mom said. "First it was my mother in Florida, who wants to know about our Christmas plans, and I told her I don't even know what's for dinner tonight. I ordered pizza, by the way. And after I hung up with the pizza guy, Aunt Abby called because Fiona wants to start gymnastics, so she was asking about a gym."

"Is she going to Tumblers?" Mia's heart sped up, but then her mom shook her head.

"They didn't have any openings, so she's looking at a place in Needham. I told her I'd have you dig out some of your old leotards to send her."

"Okay," Mia said. "But who was on the phone just now? You were talking about an offer."

Mom sighed. "That was Chet Potsworth, and—"

"Mom!" Mia stared at her. "How can you even talk to that guy? You know he's been messing with the farm to try to get Gram to sell!"

"We don't know that," Mom said.

"We do so!" Mia couldn't tell Mom how she knew. But Mom couldn't do this to Gram. "How do you think those fruit flies got in there? Magic?" Mia couldn't believe this. No wonder Mr. Potsworth hadn't tried anything else lately. With Mom on his side, he thought he'd already won. "What are you *thinking* talking to that guy?"

"I'm thinking that we have no idea who broke in with the fruit flies, *if* anyone did. I'm thinking that Gram is struggling, in more ways than one. She needs to get out from under this farm before she goes deeper into debt and loses her house." Mom put her hands on her hips and stared at Mia. "And I'm thinking you'd better watch your tone. What's gotten into you?"

"She doesn't want to sell!" Mia's voice shook. She didn't even know if that was true anymore, but she wanted it to be. Gram had always, always been there for her when she needed a hug or encouragement. Maybe Gram was frustrated enough to think about quitting, but Mia wasn't ready to let her. Ever since she heard Mr. Potsworth laughing at the processing plant, she felt as if she'd soaked up some of the fighting attitude that Gram had lost.

Mia took her signed permission slip and stomped up to her room. She wanted to throw something, but she knew that wouldn't do any good. So she did the only thing she could that might actually help Gram—worked on her Vermont Launch Junior project.

It was an hour later when Mom came and sat down on Mia's bed. "You know I'm trying to help Gram, right?"

"She doesn't want help. Why can't she make her own decisions without you talking to that guy behind her back?"

Mom nodded slowly. "You're right about that. And I already spoke with Gram about my conversation tonight."

"You did?"

"I called her when you went upstairs. She wasn't thrilled that I reached out to Mr. Potsworth. But she's going to think about his offer."

Mia shook her head. It was all so wrong. "Even if he *didn't* do all that stuff to Gram's farm, at the very least, he's being super pushy with her. He's a jerk. Doesn't that *matter* to you?"

Mom sighed. "It does matter. But selling to him may be Gram's best option." She picked up Neptune and flopped one of his wings a little. "In a perfect world, Mia, an amazing woman like Gram wouldn't have to deal with any of this. But we don't live in that world." Mom looked sad about that, and Mia felt a little of her anger leak away. "When I got my first job at a law firm, one of the partners was so dismissive of the women in the office. We'd get left out of meetings, and he'd make comments about our skirts and jokes about . . . well . . . jokes that were inappropriate."

Mia stared at her mom. She thought about Clover on the beach and Anna's mom at work in Silicon Valley. Did every woman she knew have some awful secret story? "How come you never told me about this?"

Mom shrugged. "I guess it never came up. But anyway, he was my boss, and I was young and inexperienced. I needed that job to pay back my college loans, so I dealt with it until I could move. That was what I had to do. And this . . . well, this might be what Gram has to do. It may be her best option. She'll have to decide." She looked up at Mia. "Does that make sense at all?"

Mia shrugged. Mostly it made her sad. "It's just . . . Gram's never given up on anything." She took Neptune away from Mom. "And Gram's not young or inexperienced. She knows what she's doing, and she has amazing ideas if people would just listen to her. It's not fair."

"No. It's not." Mom sighed. "I'll call you when the food gets here." She headed for the door but turned back. "Did you find any leotards for Fiona?"

"Shoot. I got working on something and forgot to check. I'll look now."

Mom left, and Mia pulled out the box full of gymnastics stuff she'd outgrown. She dug out a purple leotard, two pink ones, and the shiny blue one she'd loved best. Fiona would like that one, too. There should have been a matching hair scrunchie in there somewhere. Mia reached down to the bottom corners of the box and felt around for it.

Instead, she pulled out an Olympic pin.

Her stomach twisted, and she dropped it as if it had burned her.

She thought she had gotten rid of them all, but it must have fallen off her old gym bag. And there it was, waiting for her at the bottom of the box.

CHAPTER 16

The Story from the Bottom of the Box

The enamel pin had a bright American flag on it, with an outline of a girl on a balance beam and, above that, five delicate gold Olympic rings. It was the first pin he'd given her. He told her he'd been holding on to it for just the right person, and she'd worked so hard on the beam that she deserved it. Mia had pinned it to the gym bag she brought to practice every day.

She remembered the day Phil started at Tumblers. Everybody was excited because he'd worked with Olympic athletes during the 2012 games. They had a real live assistant Olympic gymnastics coach at their gym! He'd been a gymnast in college, too, and was still amazing at vault.

And he was just really nice. He'd been so nice. To everyone. But to Mia especially.

She looked at the pin on her floor and tried to remember when things started to feel different. She wasn't sure. But looking back now, there were so many things that seemed weird. He'd followed all the gymnasts on social media and asked for their cell phone numbers so he could text updates on practice times. He always hearted all of Mia's posts, and sometimes he'd text her even when there was no practice news. It was never anything bad or anything. Just little encouraging notes—*Hey, kiddo! Ready to go after that back handspring again on Monday?*—or funny pictures like the cat dangling from its paws on a tree limb, with a line about hanging in there and a smiley face. A few times, he sent her goofy pictures of himself. Posing with the Champ the Lake Monster statue on the waterfront. Doing a handstand in his swim trunks at the beach with the message: *You should send me a pic of you, too!* One time, Mia was already in bed when she got a text that said, *Hey there! Thinking of you tonight & looking forward to seeing you tomorrow!*

Mia stared at the pin on the floor. Regular grown-ups didn't do stuff like that. She could see that now. It was easy from a distance. Like the crickets. *Hey, maybe climb out of that water so you don't drown!* But back then, it had all just felt weird. And when Mia asked around, everybody said yeah, Phil was super friendly and kind of awkward and okay, maybe a little touchy, but that was just how Phil was. Everybody loved him. Coach Carrie was always on her gymnasts to eat healthy and lay off the junk food, but Phil would slip them Skittles and Starbursts after practice when she wasn't looking. "Our secret, okay?" He'd winked at Mia when he gave her the king-size Twix bar.

He gave a few girls pins, too, and he hugged everybody. That seemed fine at first. Coach Carrie hugged them when they left sometimes, too, and Phil was just there with her. Somebody Mia was *supposed* to hug. She didn't feel like she had a choice.

But after a while—Mia didn't even know when it changed—Phil's hugs felt weird to her. They were too tight and too pressed-up-against-her, and they lasted too long, and she couldn't really pull away, so she'd started avoiding him at the end of practice. That went on for a week, until her friends Kira and Eunice started joking about it, saying that her name, Mia, stood for Missing In Action.

Mia laughed it off. She didn't tell them she'd gone MIA on purpose, hiding out in the bathroom so she wouldn't have to hug Phil. She tried to make herself invisible so he wouldn't bother her. Like the opposite of a kung fu mantis.

That was Gram's favorite insect, other than crickets.

She'd shown Mia a video once. It was this little red-and-black praying mantis that scared off jumping spiders by standing up on its hind legs and raising its front legs, all fierce, over its head so it would look big and tough. "So any time you need some courage, you just take a deep breath and stand up tall like that little guy," Gram had told Mia, "and you'll start to feel bigger and braver, too."

But Mia had learned to make herself small. Instead of showing off at practice and celebrating with her friends, she'd stopped doing the things she was best at. She worked hard to not be noticed. She still did that sometimes, even though Phil was far away. Once you got in the habit of being small, it was hard to feel safe being your normal size anymore.

Mia reached out and picked up the pin. She took off the back and let the sharp part poke her finger. The back rubs had started not long after Phil gave her the pin. He was always offering back rubs when people were sore after a workout. And who didn't love a back rub?

But on that one day, Mia had flopped down on a chair after practice to wait for her ride, and Phil had come up behind her and said, "You must be wiped out from all that work on the bars today!" and started rubbing her shoulders. Mia couldn't even remember what changed exactly, if he was standing too close or pressing against her or breathing on her or where his hands even were, but all of a sudden, it felt icky.

Mia felt icky. And she didn't know what to do, so she said, "I should check for my ride," and started to stand up, but he kind of pushed her back down with his hands on her shoulders to keep her from leaving. Had he really pushed her down? He had. Or she would have gone to the door. And then she'd just stayed in her chair with his hands on her because she was afraid to try again, and probably she was wrong and it was nothing anyway. Coach Carrie was right there in the office. So it had to be okay. Right?

Only it wasn't. Mia still felt icky when she got home. She wasn't even sure she could say exactly what happened, but something had, and it felt gross and wrong and probably she should have said something to her mom, but how could you say something when you couldn't even explain what happened yourself? You couldn't. Mia had felt like she couldn't anyway. So she'd gone girl-cricket quiet and disappeared into her room right after dinner.

The next weekend, when it was time to go back to gymnastics, Mia still didn't feel right. She told Mom she had a stomachache, but it was almost time for the Snowflake Competition, and Mom said to go anyway and she'd probably feel better when she got there, so Mia did.

When she got to the gym, she felt worse. She needed to

practice her beam routine, but she didn't want to do that while Phil was at the beam, so she waited until he was busy at the vault with Eunice.

Mia was halfway through her routine when it was time for the back walkover. She stood on her right leg with her left leg pointed forward, perfectly balanced. But when Mia bent backward to spot the beam, she spotted him instead, walking toward her, and the next thing she knew, she was on the mat underneath the beam with her arm bent at a scary angle.

Mom was still in the building, watching through the glass—she'd been waiting to make sure Mia's stomach was okay—and she came running in and took Mia to the emergency room. There were X-rays and whispers and meetings and then surgery and recovery and TV shows and Popsicles and then more surgery and another five months of healing before Mia could even go to gym class again.

Mia turned the pin over in her hands. She couldn't even remember being the girl who felt so excited to have it on her gym bag, who thought maybe she'd go to the Olympics someday, too. Mia never thought about that after her fall. She wasn't going back to Tumblers. Not with him there. Even if he was gone, it wouldn't have worked.

Things happened fast in gymnastics. The season Mia

missed was the season she would have gotten her back layout on the floor and her giant on the bars, and by the time she could have gone back, Kira and Eunice weren't even in the same level anymore. So Mia had stuck with streaming TV shows and eating Chex Mix in her basement.

"Did you find them?" Mom appeared in the doorway.

Mia closed her fist around the pin so Mom wouldn't see it. "Yep, I have three that should fit her." With her other hand, she tossed Mom the leotards.

"Great. I'll mail these tomorrow." Mom nodded at the box. "Put that away and come down for pizza. Dad's home, and Gram decided to join us, too."

"Okay."

Mom left. Mia waited to hear her footsteps go all the way downstairs before she opened her hand and looked down at it. The pin had left marks where its sharp edges poked into the soft part of her palm. Above that, right below her fingers, her calluses had hardened up again from all her arm hangs at the gym. She'd done seventy seconds last time. Maria said she'd probably be able to make it through the rings now, but Mia wasn't sure. Sometimes she still felt like she'd left all her confidence on that mat under the balance beam, with Phil standing over it.

CHAPTER 17

Me Too

"Do we have crushed red pepper flakes?" Dad asked.

"Check behind the moose," Mom said.

"Squeeze its ear while you're over there," Gram said.

Dad found his pepper and squeezed the moose's ear, but nothing happened. "Is it supposed to say something? I can feel the little speaker thing in there, but it doesn't work." He tried the other ear, and the moose called out, "Hello from Vermont!"

"It's supposed to say two different things," Gram said. "One of your speakers must be broken. The one Bob gave me when we first moved in had the same issue. Not that I wanted a talking moose in my office anyway. I gave it to my neighbor for her preschool classroom."

"Well, somebody must like them," Mia said. "Aren't they pretty popular?"

Gram nodded. "He's a good businessman. And a decent guy. He offered to buy out my lease and take over the space if I have to close. I may ask what he thinks about this sale . . ."

"You might really do that?" Mia knew Gram was frustrated, but she still couldn't believe it.

"Mia, my dear. We've had freezer issues, humidity issues, seagulls, and fruit flies. I don't like to think of myself as a woman who gives up on anything. But I also don't like to think of myself as a fool, and I'm just not having luck with investors. If things don't turn around soon, selling may be my best option."

"I think that's smart," Mom said. "You should be enjoying life at your age. Not—"

"I *enjoy* working," Gram said. "I always have. Even in the early days. I put up with a lot when I was the only woman in UVM's entomology department for those first ten years—male colleagues taking credit for my projects, telling me to go home and raise my kids—but I still loved going to work every day."

"Well, maybe things will turn around," Mia said. "Daniel told you how much everybody loved the Chirp Challenge at the farmers market, right? And did we ever show you this?" Mia took out her phone and pulled up

Mayor Obasanjo's page with her Chirp Challenge selfie. "The mayor loves your crickets!"

Gram looked down at the phone. "Well, look at that!"

"It's been shared four hundred times, so that's pretty cool," Mia said. "And she linked to your website with info about the open house on Sunday, so maybe lots of people will see that and show up!" She didn't want Gram to give up hope. Not when Mia might actually be able to do something to help.

"You're still having that open house?" Mom sounded disappointed. "I thought with all the issues you've been having, you might call it off."

"Oh, no. I already put an ad in the paper, and we'll be okay," Gram said. "We haven't been producing like we should, but I still have three hundred pounds of frozen crickets and a batch that'll be ready to harvest soon. As long as we keep our temperature and humidity steady and don't have any freezer issues, we'll be in good shape."

"Good!" Mia said. "I bet you'll have a huge crowd."

"Maybe," Gram said. "It would be nice to have a good turnout in case this is our last hurrah." She sounded so tired. And that made Mia want to fight even harder.

They had an hour of Launch Camp before the field trip to hear the speaker on Tuesday. Everyone was racing around, trying to finish Vermont Launch Junior projects. Also stuffing their faces with food.

Aidan had spent the night before experimenting with variations on Gram's cricket-flour cookie recipes. "I figured out the perfect balance for health and deliciousness," he said.

"Did you leave out the crickets and add more chocolate chips?" Eli hollered from across the room.

"Nope," Aidan said. "I figured out you can replace twenty percent of the regular flour with cricket flour to make it healthy without messing with the texture. Any more than that and your dough gets gritty."

Mia sampled the cookies and thought they were great. So were the bao buns Quan and Bella had brought in to share. They were all soft and fluffy with sweet barbecued pork inside. Julia and Dylan were on their third servings each.

"Okay, everybody!" Zoya called. "I know you're on deadline, and it's tough to miss work time today, so I've arranged for the maker space to be open tonight if anybody wants to work for a few hours later. Any takers?"

Every hand went up, including Mia's.

"Great," Zoya said. "Let's get things cleaned up for now, and we'll head over to the college."

They walked the four blocks to UVM, where the speaker was presenting in a big lecture hall. They were the only kids there. Everybody else seemed to be enrolled in college business classes. Mia had brought her notebook to brainstorm in case Anne Marie Spangler's talk was boring, but it turned out to be great. She talked about how she'd built her first business—a small start-up in Vermont—and then sold it to a bigger company so she could launch another one and eventually ended up running her multimillion-dollar company called Five Dogs Apparel. When Anne Marie Spangler talked about her business plan, Mia felt pretty cool that she had done almost all the same things in her plan for Gram's farm.

After the talk, Zoya gave them fifteen minutes to use the bathroom and look around the art gallery in the building before they walked back to camp. Mia was waiting for Clover to come out of the ladies' room when she heard some college students still talking with the guest speaker, so she wandered back into the lecture hall.

"Without a doubt, you ladies will face challenges your male colleagues don't have to deal with," Anne Marie Spangler told them. "My first job out of college was a nightmare because the guy who ran my department couldn't keep his hands to himself."

Mia moved a little closer and slipped into one of the seats. Anne Marie was talking quietly, but Mia could still hear as she told the young women how her boss had harassed her at work every day. It was pretty awful.

"So what did you do?" one of the students asked.

"Eventually, I quit," Anne Marie answered. "I found a different job."

"That's not right," the other student said. "He's the one who should have had to leave."

"Yep. But that's how things worked back then. Welcome to the patriarchy." Then Anne Marie Spangler waved her hand through the air as if the patriarchy were a fruit fly she could flick away. "It worked out, though. Last year, I bought his company and fired him."

"That's epic," one of the students said.

"Anne Marie?" a voice called from the lobby. "Your car's here."

The students thanked her and left, and Anne Marie Spangler started packing up her computer. Mia watched her fold the cord and tuck it into her briefcase. Anne Marie looked so . . . normal. She looked fine. Like that stuff never happened to her. How did she do that? Mia wanted to ask, but she felt stuck in her chair, and her voice was all gummed up in her throat.

Anne Marie zipped her briefcase, tossed it over her shoulder, and turned to leave. "Oh!" she said. "I'm sorry. I didn't see you there. Did you have one last question?"

Mia nodded.

Anne Marie looked at her, waiting.

"It's not a question, actually," Mia said. "I just . . ." She blinked fast. "That kind of happened to me, too."

Anne Marie tipped her head, confused.

"That thing you talked about. With your boss."

"Ohh." She put her briefcase down and gestured to the chair next to Mia. "Okay if I sit with you for a minute?"

Mia nodded.

"I'm so sorry something like that happened to you."

Mia nodded again. "Me too."

"Do you want to talk any more about it?"

"No," Mia said. Then she added, "It wasn't as bad as what happened to you. But . . ."

"Just because it could have been worse doesn't make it all right," Anne Marie said. "It wasn't okay."

"No," Mia said. "No." She said it again. Louder. "No. It wasn't okay."

"Did you talk with your parents about what happened?"

Mia shook her head. Until now, she'd never said anything to anybody. Because everybody loved Phil, and at first she'd been too confused and afraid to say anything. Then later, it seemed too late to speak up. She should have said something right away. It was weird to talk about it now. Wasn't it? It shouldn't matter anymore anyway. But it did.

"It was a long time ago," Mia finally said. "It's not anybody I see now."

"So you're safe," Anne Marie said.

Mia nodded.

"Anne Marie?" The lady from the car popped her head in again. "We need to head out if you're going to catch this flight."

"Okay." She looked back at Mia. "When something like this happens, it can be a lot to sort out. But you'll be okay. You really will. Do think about talking to your family or another adult you trust, though. It might help."

Mia nodded one last time, even though she couldn't do that. Not now. She couldn't even figure out why she'd said something to this stranger lady she was never going to see again.

Maybe that was why she said it.

Or maybe it was because she'd been so surprised that people who looked and talked and ran companies like Anne Marie had stuff happen to them, too.

CHAPTER 18

Disasters and Spies

That afternoon at Warrior Camp, instead of heading over to hang on her usual bar, Mia lined up for the rings.

"All right!" Maria gave her a high five. "You've been working so hard, you're going to fly through these."

"I'm going to give it a try, at least." Mia jumped from the mat to the first two rings, which were pretty close together. That was the easy part. Then she took a deep breath, let go of the ring behind her, and let her body weight swing her forward to grab the next one.

"Great! Keep that momentum!" Maria shouted.

Mia let go again and grabbed the next ring. She made it almost to the end, but the last ring was too far away. She reached for it but missed and found herself swinging from one arm. She kicked her feet, grabbed the ring with her other hand, and held on. But now she was swinging all over the place and didn't have the right momentum at all. She was about to drop when Maria called out, "Reach back now and steady yourself! You've got this!"

Mia's arms were on fire. She could feel the taped rings tugging at the skin on her calluses and really didn't want to rip them open again. But she thought about reaching back. She thought about how free and strong she used to feel, jumping off those high red rocks at the lake. Splashing into the cool, clear water and staring up at the summer-blue sky.

Maybe she would never be that brave, lake-rocks Mia again. But she could reach back and borrow some courage from her. Maybe she couldn't go back to Boston and buy Tumblers and get rid of Phil. But she was going to get that last ring.

Mia's hands burned, but she held on. She kept her grip and waited until she wasn't swinging anymore. Then she let go with one hand and reached back for the ring behind her.

"That's it!" Maria shouted. "Now give a pull to get yourself going again. Big swing!"

"You got this, Mia!" Clover shouted.

Mia pulled but didn't move all that much. So she pulled

harder. She did it again, and when she started swinging—really swinging—she let go with her back hand, reached forward as far as she could, and felt the rough tape of the last ring on her palm. She grabbed it, swung forward once more, and landed on the mat at the end of the course.

The whole gym exploded in applause.

Mia looked down at her hands. They were red and raw and stinging in the best possible way.

Clover ran up and hugged her. Isaac and Liam were right behind her with high fives.

"Want to try the warped wall now?" Isaac asked. He'd started wearing his hair in a ponytail, so she could finally tell him apart from Liam.

"Sure!" Mia was on a roll. Why not?

The warped wall didn't go quite as well. Mia didn't even get to eight feet on her first try, but by the time Maria blew her whistle at the end of camp, she was almost to the ten-foot line.

"You were on fire today," Clover said as they walked down the hallway to the cricket farm. They'd promised to help Daniel with feeding and watering before they went back to Launch Camp for the late work session. "You'll be on top of that wall in no time!"

"I hope so," Mia said. And she meant that. It was funny. When Warrior Camp had started, she'd looked up at that wall and thought, *No way!* But Clover had been working on it all summer. She'd made it to the top last week and looked so triumphant when she rang the bell that, just for a minute, Mia had imagined herself up there, too. "I should have tried it sooner." Mia pulled open the door to the cricket farm. "Now I only have one more week to— Ugh! Why is it so hot in here?"

Daniel was just running into the warehouse with a big fan. "Oh good!" he said. "You're here. They need water, pronto!"

Mia dropped her gym bag and grabbed a water dish from the closest bin. It was completely dry. "What happened?"

Daniel opened a window and plugged in the fan. "Thermostat was cranked up when I came in ten minutes ago," he shouted over the whirring. "Nobody was in this morning, so I have no idea how long it's been like this. We've lost about twenty percent of the adults already." He opened another window. "But if we get them water and get it cooled down quickly, we should be able to keep it to that."

Mia and Clover worked as fast as they could. While they dealt with the water, Daniel worked to harvest a bin of crickets. Mia thought about how much faster Anna's robot harvester would be. She hadn't tried it with actual crickets yet, but Mia had brought one of the cardboard condos to camp, and it seemed like it was going to work.

She couldn't wait to tell Gram but had decided it would be best to wait until after Vermont Launch Junior. Especially now, with the mess in the warehouse today.

Within an hour, all the cricket bins had fresh water, and the place was feeling cooler. "What's next?" Mia asked.

"Nothing else we can do at this point," Daniel said. "Just help me get these into the freezer and— Oh no." His voice sank.

Mia rushed over to the big chest freezer in the back of the warehouse. "Now what?"

"Looks like we blew another fuse." Daniel stared into the freezer.

"Or somebody turned it off on purpose," Mia said, looking at Daniel. This wasn't an accident. She knew it wasn't. Had Daniel turned off Gram's freezer himself?

"Can you tell how long it's been off?" Clover asked. "Maybe they're still okay . . ."

Daniel lifted a tub of what should have been frozen crickets from the freezer and pulled off the lid. They were all thawed and soupy. He cursed under his breath.

"Are all of Gram's frozen crickets in here?" Mia asked.

"Most of them," Daniel said. "She's got another freezer at home, but this was everything we harvested in the past month." He shook his head. Mia watched him. He really did seem upset. "I'm going to take today's batch to my apartment and get them into the freezer there. You can head out. Thanks for the help."

Mia fought back tears as they rode to school for the work session. She didn't know if Daniel was sabotaging Gram or if Mr. Potsworth was working by himself, but it was awful and so, so unfair. Gram had worked so hard. She'd pushed through so much and had this amazing career in a field that was almost all men. She'd built her department at the college so other women could study entomology, too. Gram had done such amazing work. How come nothing could go right for her now that she was following her dream with this farm?

When they got back to camp, Anna was excited about a change she'd made to the robot harvester—something about a six-cycle repeat. Mia tried to listen but couldn't focus.

"Don't you realize how much more efficient this is going to be?" Anna asked.

"I'm sorry." Mia explained what had just happened at the farm. "It's freaky," she said. "We were talking at my house last night about how everything was in good shape unless there were temperature or humidity issues or something went wrong with the freezer, and then bam! We have temperature and freezer issues today."

"That's what makes me think Daniel must be involved," Clover said.

Mia nodded. "I know. He's, like, Gram's favorite person, but . . ." She shook her head.

"Who was there when you were talking about that stuff?" Anna asked.

"Just my parents and Gram."

"Any chance your parents are involved?" Anna asked.

"No." Mia had thought about that. Mom really wanted Gram to sell the place, but there was no way she'd be that awful. "But I swear, if it wasn't Daniel, somebody else must have heard that conversation."

"You don't have one of those nanny cams at your house, do you?" Anna asked.

"What's that?"

"A camera that parents set up to spy on the nanny. It's usually hidden in a teddy bear or something. Lots of people have them and don't realize how easy it is to hack into them once they're set up."

"We don't have a nanny," said Mia, "or any of those spy cameras, so it's— Wait. Did you say they're hidden in teddy bears?"

"Yeah. Why? Was there a creepy teddy bear hanging around when you were talking?"

"No," Mia said. She didn't even have her teddy bear from when she was little. Neptune was the only stuffed animal she'd kept. But then she remembered the moose.

She thought about all the family conversations that had happened in the kitchen, where she'd left it. What she was thinking sounded too weird to be possible. She said it anyway. "But we have a creepy moose."

Clover gasped. "I thought something was off about that moose guy!"

Anna listened while Mia explained about the talking moose Mr. Jacobson had given her and how she'd left it in the kitchen. "But I can't imagine it's got a spy camera inside," Mia said. "The moose isn't exactly high tech. When my dad tried to make it talk, one of its ear speakers didn't even work, so I don't think—"

"Wait!" Anna held up a hand. Her fingernails were black with pink polka dots today. "Your dad squeezed the ear? And felt something in there?"

Mia nodded. "Just a broken speaker. The same thing happened with Gram's moose."

"Your grandma got a creepy moose, too?" Clover asked.

"Yeah." Mia's head was spinning. "And her moose had a broken speaker, too."

"What if those aren't broken speakers?" Anna said. "What if they're listening devices?"

"Somebody put a bug under a desk in a book I read once," Clover said. "It's totally a thing criminals do."

"Where'd you get that moose again?" Anna asked.

Mia told her more about Mr. Jacobson. "But he's always helping Gram," she said. "And why would he want her farm to fail? He hasn't tried to buy it or anything."

"Maybe *he's* working with Potsworth," Clover said. "Just because somebody acts friendly doesn't mean he's a good guy,"

"Yeah." Mia knew that.

"Where are those moose right now?" Anna asked.

"Mine's in our kitchen. Gram gave hers away to a preschool a while ago."

"Good," Anna said. "If somebody's listening to that one, all they're hearing is 'The Wheels on the Bus' and the alphabet song. But can you bring yours to camp tomorrow?"

"I guess." That felt creepy to Mia if the moose was really listening to things. But it couldn't be, right? If an eavesdropping moose showed up in some TV spy movie, she'd laugh at how dumb it was. Even Clover's weirdest mystery-novel villains had more sensible ideas than that. "Do you really think this is possible?"

"Maybe," Anna said. "Bring it in and I can tell you for sure."

Mia felt creeped out again. "But if it might be a bug, shouldn't I smash its ear with a rock or something and break it so it doesn't work anymore?"

"No!" Clover said. "If you do that, whoever planted it will know that you know, and he'll be able to destroy whatever other evidence is out there to tie him to the crime."

"She's right," Anna said. "If this turns out to be a bug, we can use that to our advantage to figure out what's really going on. But we can only do that if the person who planted it *thinks* everything is fine." She turned to Mia. "You understand what this means, right?"

Mia's skin crawled. "My moose is a double agent now, so I have to let it keep listening to us in the kitchen?"

"Just for tonight," Anna said. "Then bring it in tomorrow and we'll figure out what's up."

"Be careful," Clover added. "Don't say anything about anything in front of the moose."

CHAPTER 19

The Moose Has Ears

Everybody got home late that night, so dinner was sandwiches on the couch. Mia was relieved she didn't have to deal with the eavesdropping moose until it was time to do dishes.

"You had a busy day," Mom said. "How was that speaker you went to see this morning?"

"Good," Mia said. "She talked about her businesses and everything." That wasn't what Mia would remember most about Anne Marie, but she wasn't ready to talk to Mom about that. And she sure didn't want to talk about it in front of the moose. "How was your preliminary hearing today?" That seemed like a safer conversation. Maybe they could bore the moose to death.

"Well, it was complicated," Mom said, and went on about some motion for something to be dismissed and why it might not be. Mia nodded and dried the plates. When she was finished, she took the moose up to her room.

She didn't want the moose up there, but she also didn't want Mom or Dad to say something important in front of it, so she shoved it deep into one of the boxes in her closet and got ready for bed. She didn't get much sleep. She was too creeped out about the moose maybe listening to her breathe.

"Bringing a friend today?" Mom asked when Mia plopped the moose down beside her in the car the next morning.

"I thought I'd share it as an example of a successful product." That was the plan if anybody asked about the moose at Launch Camp, too. It was easier than trying to explain that they thought it might be a spy.

"Have fun!" Mom said when she dropped Mia off. Clover and Anna were waiting at the door.

"That's it, huh?" Anna said.

"Yep." Mia held out the moose.

"That's super cute," Clover said. "No wonder they've been so successful." She gave Mia a look that said "obviously-the-moose-is-terrible-but-don't-forget-to-play-along-with-this-because-it-might-be-listening."

"Right," Mia said.

They took the moose inside and got set up at a maker-space table. Anna scribbled a note and slid it across the table.

Keep talking about how cool the moose is while I work on this.

Mia and Clover nodded. Anna picked up a tiny pair of scissors and started snipping stitches on the moose's ear.

"So," Mia said. "It's a pretty great moose, right?" She was a terrible moose faker.

"It's neat that they talk." Clover reached out and squeezed the ear Anna wasn't cutting open.

"Hello from Vermont!" the moose called out, just as Anna pulled a half-dollar-size electronic-looking thing out of its other ear.

Mia grabbed the pen.

Can you tell what it is?

Anna turned the round thing over in her hands for a few seconds and then nodded. Mia handed her the pen.

Definitely a small listening/transmitting device. I've seen this kind before.

Keep talking while I take out the SD card.

"So," Mia said. "What do you think you'll try at Warrior Camp tomorrow?"

Clover said something about the spider wall, but Mia wasn't paying attention because her eyes were glued to the tiny rectangle Anna had just ejected from the moose's ear recorder. Anna popped the card into her laptop and put the rest of the recorder back in the moose's ear.

"Hey, Mia!" Anna said. "Could I take your moose home to show my mom? I think she'd like to order one for my cousin's birthday."

"Uh . . . sure," Mia said.

"Thanks," Anna said. "I'll put it with my stuff in the other room so I don't forget." She held up an I'll-be-right-back finger and left with the moose.

"Okay, now we can talk," Anna said when she returned, mooseless. "The actual listening device is back in the moose, and it's probably still transmitting to . . . wherever it's transmitting. But I have the recording card here. Check this out." She clicked a play button on the laptop screen, and Mia heard her father's voice.

"She's thankful it wasn't some other insect that carries cricket diseases."

Then Mia heard herself. *"There are cricket diseases?"*

And Dad again. *"Apparently. She was telling me about this virus called . . . what was it?"*

Then Mom. *"CPV."*

Mia stared at the laptop. She looked up at Anna and Clover. "This is all from our kitchen!"

They listened while Dad-on-the-recorder explained how devastating that virus could be to a cricket farm and how that had just happened to a farm in Quebec.

Anna fast-forwarded to another spot on the recording, and Mia heard Gram's voice.

"As long as we keep our temperature and humidity steady and don't have any freezer issues, we'll be in good shape."

"Both of those things went wrong the very next day!" Mia's head was spinning. "And you said this thing hasn't just been recording? There's been somebody *listening* to us in our house whenever we talk?"

"Not every second, probably, but yeah," Anna said. "My guess is that they're also recording at the remote location. So this card would just be a backup."

Mia wanted to throw up. But then she thought about Mr. Jacobson, giving her that moose, saying he had it made especially for her. She thought about how he was always showing up to "help" Gram, when really he'd been working with Chet Potsworth the whole time. And the queasiness in her stomach hardened into something else. What kind of terrible person would do that? She wanted to rip that stupid moose's ear right off and smash the recorder into a million pieces. But she couldn't. "So what am I supposed to do now? Take that thing home and pretend there's not some creep spying on my family?"

"Not yet," Anna said. "I'll take it home tonight because I have an idea. But then, yeah . . . you need to take it back and pretend everything's fine. In order for this to work, this Jacobson guy can't find out that we know. But trust me. If we do this right, he'll get what's coming to him."

Anna brought the moose back to camp on Thursday. She left it in the hallway so they could talk about it.

"Is the listening device still in there?" Mia asked.

"Yep," Anna said, "but I also added my own recorder. Prima helped me set it up so—"

"Wait—so now *you're* going to spy on me, too? How's that supposed to help?"

"It'll help because the moose isn't going to stay with you," Anna said. "It's going back where it came from. You said Mr. Jacobson has an office with a shelf full of moose, right? Do you think you can get in there and swap out your moose for one of the others?"

"You want me to break in to the moose office now?" Mia had practically had a heart attack when they almost got caught in the food-processing plant. She shook her head. "No way."

"You won't have to break in," Clover said.

"I'm not doing that again," Mia said. "We could have gotten arrested!"

"I know, I know," Clover said. "But this time, we won't enter without permission, either. We'll just stop by to visit. He likes you, right?"

"He pretends to."

"So we can all go together." Clover looked over at Anna, who nodded. "We'll tell him we need advice from a successful entrepreneur. Then two of us can distract him while the other one swaps out the moose."

Mia ran through that scenario in her head. It seemed slightly less terrifying than the processing plant ordeal. It also seemed like it might work. And there was nothing Mia wanted more than to see Mr. Jacobson and Mr. Potsworth get caught. "Okay."

"Good," Clover said. "We'll do it this weekend." She pulled out her laptop. "And now we need to get ready for Vermont Launch Junior."

The maker space was a flurry of activity. Eli and Nick were trying to get KicksFinder into the app store before they had to present. Quan and Bella still had to edit their business plan. Aidan was writing up Cookies for a Cause recipe cards. Dylan and Julia were working on the display board for their jewelry.

Anna's cricket-harvesting robot was mostly ready, but she was working on a few last-minute changes. Mia had brought in a tub of crickets for testing, and sometimes the arm got glitchy and pivoted back and forth, flinging crickets around. Anna thought she could get that fixed, but she said it was fine even if it was still a little wonky. Prototypes were always like that, and as long as the basic idea was there, they'd be okay.

Mia and Clover had finished most of the competition requirements but had to race through the rest. They'd done pretty well for starting so late, though. Mia was in a great mood by the time Launch Camp wrapped up.

Then she went out to the hallway and remembered the moose.

CHAPTER 20

The Truth about Tumblers

Mia left the moose in her gym bag during Warrior Camp. She did the rings again and tried the warped wall but kept banging her knee because she couldn't concentrate.

"Come on, warrior!" Maria called as Mia slid down. "Focus!"

The problem was, Mia had too much to focus on. Gram's troubles at the farm and Vermont Launch Junior and the spying moose she had to carry around now.

When Mia got home, she took the moose straight to her closet and stuffed it into the bottom of a box, under a heap of old Halloween costumes. She had dinner with her parents and talked a little about Vermont Launch Junior. Families were allowed to be in the audience, but thankfully, her mom and dad agreed to skip that. Mia had told them it would make her too nervous, and that was true.

It was also true that Mia didn't want Mom to know what she and Clover had been working on. Mom would just start in again about how it was time for Gram to retire. She'd laugh at Mia's plan or, worse, do that thing that adults do where they smile because they think something is cute instead of an actual serious project that you've worked hard to prepare.

And they had worked hard. They had Saturday's presentation all planned out. Mia's introduction would talk about how insects are a healthy, sustainable protein. Clover would talk about their social media campaign, and Anna would demonstrate the harvesting robot. They had samples to give out, too. Gram had made a batch of barbecue crickets that were really great, so Mia chose those and the sea salt and garlic to share. Gram was so distracted lately that she hadn't even asked what they were for.

Mia couldn't stop thinking about that as she got ready for bed. It was hard to believe this ready-to-call-it-a-day Gram was the same person who'd been so excited to show off the cricket farm to her family just a month ago. And it was all because of those awful men and their rotten spying moose. They'd taken away all Gram's excitement for something she loved so much. Who did they think they were?

Mia flung back her covers, got out of bed, and dug the

moose out of the box. She stared at it, and a hard knot of anger tightened in her chest. She knew she had to leave it alone or their plan wouldn't work. But she wanted to shred it to threads and stuff them into Mr. Jacobson's stupid, lying mouth. What kind of terrible person pretended to be nice to somebody just so they could hurt them?

Mia's fingernails dug into the plush moose.

Her eyes stung with tears. She knew what kind.

She dropped the moose on the floor and dragged another box out of the closet. She shoved her hand way down through the wrinkled leotards and sweatshirts and felt around. Where was it? She pulled out trophies and T-shirts and ribbons and warm-up jackets. She pulled out exhibition programs and athletic tape and the towel they gave everybody at the Snowflake Competition the year she was nine.

And then there it was at the bottom of the box.

I've been holding on to this for just the right person.

You work so hard on the beam.

You deserve it.

No, Mia thought.

No.

She hadn't deserved any of it.

She wanted that pin out of her room. Out of her house. She wanted it out of the world.

Mia squeezed her fist tight around the pin and opened

her door. Her parents were in their room—she could hear the TV—so she crept past and went downstairs. She opened the kitchen door, let it close slowly so it wouldn't slam, and stepped onto the porch.

A jigsaw puzzle of a moon was shining through the branches of the neighbor's oak tree, lighting up Mom's garden with the rock wall. The crickets were chirping. The males, anyway. Mia wanted to scream at all those quiet female crickets.

Say something!

Chirp!

Mia walked barefoot through the cool grass. She pulled a big, flat rock off the garden wall onto the lawn and set the pin on top of it, right in the center. She had felt so special with that pin.

All the way from the Olympics.

Just the right person.

Mia grabbed another rock and knelt in the damp grass. She lifted the rock high over her head and smashed it down onto the pin as hard as she could. Shards of enamel flew into the grass. Mia let them go. She lifted the rock and brought it down again.

You deserve it.

Again and again, until all that was left was a bent-up, scratched metal post and a pile of dust.

Mia blew it away.

She sat back, breathing hard. The hair around her temples was damp with sweat. She hadn't even noticed she was crying until a breeze swept in and cooled the tears on her cheeks.

Mia took a long, deep breath of dark, quiet air. She stood up and put the rocks back on her mother's garden wall.

Then she went back inside to bed. And slept.

Mia was having cereal when her mom came downstairs Friday morning. "You're an early bird today," Mom said.

Mia nodded. "Last day of Launch Camp before the competition." Zoya had added a Friday session so they'd have one more day to work.

"We need to leave a little early to pick up Gram, okay? I'm taking her to an eye doctor appointment after I drop you off."

"I'll be ready in, like, five minutes."

"I'm so glad you decided to do that camp." Mom poured a cup of coffee. "And oh! Did I tell you that it looks like Fiona will get to go to Tumblers after all?"

"What?" Mia's cereal felt like sawdust in her mouth.

"Fiona got into Tumblers! Isn't that great?"

Mia couldn't answer. Her heart was pounding so fast, she thought it might burst out and keep going right through the kitchen door.

"They had a last-minute opening." Mom kept going. "Aunt Abby says Fiona won't stop talking about it. Just like Mia, she says. She's going to compete on the beam, just like Mia." When Mia still didn't say anything, Mom said, "Are you okay?"

Mia forced herself to swallow the cereal, but it stuck in her throat. Finally, she managed, "I'm fine. Just nervous about the competition."

"You're going to be great," Mom said. "Let me get dressed, and we'll get you to camp."

Mia dumped her cereal in the trash, went to her room, and packed up her folder for Vermont Launch Junior. She didn't have to bring the moose to camp today. The plan was for her, Anna, and Clover to visit Gram at the cricket farm after dinner and sneak it into Mr. Jacobson's office then. But Mia couldn't think about that now. All she could think about was Fiona.

Phil was still there. Mia knew because she still looked at the Tumblers website sometimes and saw pictures of him with the kids at competitions. He'd be smiling his goofy smile and giving the thumbs-up or posing with his arm around somebody. Mia would study the girls' faces and wonder if they felt the way she had when Phil hugged her too long or texted her late at night or gave her that weird back rub. Was she the only one? Mia always wondered.

And now Fiona was going to train with him.

"Mia! Ready to go?" Mom called up.

Mia went downstairs and got in the car. It was supposed to be ninety today, and the car was already sweltering. Mom turned on the AC and the radio, and Mia looked out the window. She had to say something. But she'd waited so long. Would Mom even believe her? Would she think Mia was making a big deal out of nothing?

It didn't matter. She had to say something. Fiona couldn't go there.

Except now they were at Gram's house already.

"Good morning!" Gram climbed into the front seat. She turned to look at Mia. "How's my favorite granddaughter?"

"Fine," Mia lied, and waited for Gram to turn back around. But she didn't. She kept looking at Mia. She could always tell when Mia wasn't okay. And Mia wasn't okay. Not at all. But she couldn't do this right now. She opened her folder and looked down to keep from crying.

"Any idea how long this appointment might last?" Mom asked Gram. "If there's time, I'm going to run to the post office before I pick you up. Mia's cousin is starting gymnastics, so we're sending her some hand-me-down leotards."

Mia's heart raced. She tried to calm herself. It was okay. Mom could mail the leotards. There would still be time to tell her what happened before Fiona went for her first class. Wouldn't there? Mia swallowed hard. "When is Fiona starting at Tumblers?"

"Tomorrow morning!" Mom said. "That spot opened up just in time for the new session. Isn't that great luck?"

"No!" Mia blurted it out before she could think.

"What?" Mom stopped at a red light and looked in the rearview mirror. By then Mia was sobbing. "Mia, what's wrong?"

"Fiona can't go to Tumblers!"

Gram reached back and took her hand just as the light turned green.

"Mia . . ." Mom looked around and pulled into a convenience store parking lot. She parked way over at the side where there were no other cars. Then she turned to Mia. "What's going on? Why are you saying this?"

Mia swallowed hard. She didn't let go of Gram's hand. She needed all the strength she could get. Her stomach twisted, and her mouth was dry, but she had to make the words come out. Fiona couldn't go there. And Mia was the only one who knew why.

"Because of Phil," she said, finally looking up at Mom. "He's creepy, and when I was there, he . . . he did stuff."

"Oh, honey . . ." Gram squeezed her hand. She didn't say anything else. She just held on.

Mom bit her lip. She took a long breath. Then she reached back and took Mia's other hand. "Tell me what happened."

And so Mia did. While people came in and out of the store with their morning coffee, Mia told everything. About the texts and the pins and the hugs and the weird creepy back rub she tried to walk away from and got pushed back down and how the next day, she'd been afraid to see him, and then when she did she fell off the beam.

"Oh, Mia . . ." Mom's eyes filled with tears. "I am so, so sorry. I remember you didn't want to go that day. I had no idea."

"Because I didn't tell you," Mia said.

Mom nodded. "I wish you had."

"I was afraid nobody would believe me," Mia said quietly.

"I'll always believe you, Mia."

"But you didn't believe Gram when she said someone was trying to sabotage her farm."

"That's not—" Mom stopped. She blinked fast and then looked out the window, where a lady was trying to get her toddler buckled into a minivan car seat. Mom sighed. "You're right. I didn't know what was going on with the farm, but . . . I was wrong." She looked at Gram. "I should have believed you. I'm sorry. I really am."

Gram patted Mom's hand and said, "That's okay. And this isn't quite the same anyway." She turned to Mia. "Mia, your mom and dad are the best people I know. You can trust them with things like this."

"And you can always talk to Gram, too," Mom said. "We all love you so much."

"I know." Mia unbuckled her seat belt, leaned forward, and let Mom wrap her in an awkward half hug. Gram wrapped her arms around both of them, too. It felt so good, and warm, and safe. Finally, Mia pulled back and looked at Mom. "Will you talk to Aunt Abby about Fiona?"

Mom nodded. "As soon as I get home. And I'm going to call Coach Carrie. She needs to know about this immediately."

"What if he says it's not true?" Mia's stomach twisted again. Everybody loved Phil. Maybe Mom and Gram believed Mia, but would anybody else? "What if he says I'm making a big deal out of nothing? What if nobody believes me?"

"This isn't nothing." Now Mom looked angry. "I know Coach Carrie, and she'll take this seriously. The gym will investigate, and they'll talk with other families, too. I hope I'm wrong about this, Mia, but when an adult is inappropriate like this, it's rarely with just one kid." She took a shaky breath. "He's probably done the same to other girls. Or worse."

Mia's heart sank. "Because I didn't say anything." How could she not have thought of that? "If that happened— if he hurt somebody else, it's all my fault!"

"No!" Mom said. "It's his fault. No one else's. Mia, people who come after kids like this are experts at manipulating them. Making them think they need to stay quiet. But you spoke up." Mom hugged her again. "That was incredibly brave, and I'm so, so proud of you. Lots of people go their whole lives without talking about things like this." Mom's voice broke a little when she said that, and her eyes filled with tears again. She'd told Mia a little about what happened at her first law firm, but this made Mia wonder if there was more. If Mom had her own pin hidden away in a box somewhere.

"You were brave before you spoke up, too," Gram said quietly, taking Mia's hand again. "You've been carrying around what happened all this time, getting up every morning, going to school, going to camp, making friends. Do you realize how brave *that* is?"

"That's not brave." Mia looked at Gram. "I just had to do that stuff."

"That's what brave women do. We keep going. Somehow we manage to grieve over things that have happened to us at the same time we're saving the world and running businesses and practicing law and raising families." Gram nodded at Mom.

"And being warriors," Mom added. "And getting ready for competitions."

"Sometimes courage is quiet," Gram said. "You were brave to speak up today, Mia. But you were brave before that, too. Sometimes getting up in the morning and being you, no matter what's happened to you and no matter what anybody says, is the bravest, most defiant thing a woman can do."

"Sometimes I'm not sure what being me even means anymore," Mia said quietly.

"Join the club," Mom said, and gave her a sad smile.

Gram smiled, too, and put a hand on Mom's shoulder. "We all have to figure that out over and over again, kiddo. That's okay."

Mia's phone dinged with a text then.

It was Clover.

ARE YOU COMING????

Mia looked at the car clock. She was fifteen minutes late for Launch Camp. They had so much work to do. And she'd already missed out on enough. She took a deep breath and wiped her face with her sleeve. She put one hand on Mom's shoulder and one on Gram's. "Thanks," she said. "For everything. But can we go now? I want to get to camp."

CHAPTER 21

Countdown to Launch

"Mia!" Clover practically tackled her in a hug when she walked into camp. "Thank God you're here! Were you trying to give us a heart attack?"

"Sorry," Mia said. "I was talking to my mom about some stuff."

"Everything okay?" Anna asked.

"I think so," Mia said, picturing Fiona in her shiny blue leotard. Aunt Abby was so protective there was no way she'd send her to Tumblers now. "It will be."

"Good," Clover said, unfolding a giant trifold poster board. "I got everything put together last night. What do you think?"

"That's amazing!" Mia turned to Anna. "And you'll bring the robot tomorrow, right?"

Anna nodded and gave the robot a pat on its claw. "Still tweaking a few things, but she's mostly ready."

Everybody spent the first part of Launch Camp on last-minute project details. Aidan had spent all his time perfecting his Cookies for a Cause recipes, so he was freaking out, trying to get his poster put together. Zoya was helping Julia and Dylan proofread their business plan. Quan and Bella were texting their dad to see if he could pick up paper plates and napkins. Eli and Nick were the only ones not racing to finish. They were sitting at a table with their poster board, eating bao buns and cookie samples.

"Anna, don't you wish you'd stayed with us?" Eli called over. "You'd be finished now."

"Doubt it," Anna hollered back at him without missing a beat. "It's hard to get anything done when certain people won't leave you alone to do your work."

Clover high-fived her and called over, "Also, she'd rather change the world than sit on her butt eating cookies."

"Hey!" Aidan looked offended.

"Even amazing cookies," Clover added quickly. "Besides . . ." She took one of the crunchy oatmeal raisin samples he'd brought in to share. "We can eat cookies *and* make the world better. Right?" She high-fived Mia.

"Right," Mia said. "And thanks. I never would have

done all this without you two." They'd finished almost all the competition requirements. They just had to write their reflections, and Anna and Clover were sleeping over tonight so they could do that—and so they could carry out their top-secret spy-moose plan.

By the time they left camp, it was after noon, and heat radiated up from the bike path. "We should stop for lunch and eat by the lake," Clover said.

They all texted their moms, who said that was fine, so the girls stopped at Mountain Mart, picked up sandwiches, and rode to the beach with the red rocks. They found a little shade along one rocky ledge, kicked off their flip-flops, and ate with their feet in the water.

By the time they finished their sandwiches, the sun was in Mia's eyes. "It's *so* hot today," she said.

Clover jumped up. "Let's swim!"

"But we don't have swimsuits."

"So?" Clover looked up and down the empty beach. She climbed to one of the medium-high rocks that jutted out over deeper water, peeled off her T-shirt, and jumped in the lake in her shorts and sports bra. "Come on!" she called when she surfaced. "It's awesome!"

Anna laughed and scrambled up the rock, too. She cannonballed in with all her clothes on, giving Clover a good splash. "Mia, come on!" Anna said. "It feels so good in here!"

Mia looked up at the rock. She wanted to do it, but she couldn't. She tried reaching back, tried to remember the girl with the rainbow swimsuit and all the courage, but it wasn't quite enough. She shook her head.

"You don't have to jump," Clover called. "Wade in. There's a nice flat path by that ledge."

So Mia stood up and shuffled into the water. It was slippery, and she was afraid she might fall, so she took tiny careful steps until finally, she was in up to her hips. Then she dove forward and plunged in headfirst. The icy water took her breath away but not in a bad way. In a whoa-wake-up, alive kind of way.

Mia gasped when she came up. "It's so cold!"

Clover grinned. "You get used to it fast." She dove under and came up between Mia and Anna. "I can't believe I just met you two this summer," she said. "It feels like we've been friends longer."

"I know." Mia turned and floated on her back, staring into the sky until the bright sun made her eyes water. She closed them and felt its warmth through her lids.

"Hey, look at this!" Anna called. She'd climbed onto a giant tree that was half-submerged in the lake. When she stood up on it, it sank down a little, so it looked like she was standing on the water. She stretched her hands into the sky.

"You're queen of the tree!" Clover shouted.

"Come be queens with me!" Anna called back, so Mia and Clover swam over and scrambled onto the tree, too. As soon as they stood up, Clover started bouncing. Mia wobbled, and for a second, she felt that panicky, heart-racing feeling. But then she caught herself. It was okay if she lost her balance and fell. She'd just splash into the lake. She wasn't going to get hurt.

Mia bounced with Clover, and Anna joined in until they were all wobbling and laughing so hard that people on the bike path were stopping to watch.

Clover waved to an old lady on a pink bike and shouted, "We're queens of this tree!"

The old lady called back, "Have fun, girls!" and rode away.

"Let's jump off together!" Clover grabbed Anna's and Mia's hands. "On the count of three. Ready?"

They bounced one . . . two . . . three times and then leaped into the clear, cold water. They splashed and floated a while longer until Clover heard her phone ding with a text back on the rocks. "That's probably the moms, checking in."

"We should head back anyway," Mia said. They still had to write up their reflections and get out to the industrial park before Mr. Jacobson left for the day at five.

Mia's clothes were soaked, and her wet hair dripped into her eyes as she put on her bike helmet, but she didn't care. Cooling off and goofing around with Anna and Clover had given her a burst of energy.

When the girls got to Mia's house, they holed up in her bedroom finishing the written parts of the project. Mia played her Renegade Kickboxers playlist extra loud while they worked so the moose in her closet couldn't hear what they were talking about.

"There!" Mia said, printing out the final pages. "We're as ready as we'll ever be."

"We're *almost* ready," Anna said, reaching for her backpack. She pulled out seven different bottles of nail polish. "We need matching manicures."

"Ohh! I love it!" Clover said. "What color do we want?"

Mia picked up a sparkly green. "How about this one? Since crickets are earth-friendly."

"Perfect!" Anna said. "And let's do a lightning bolt down the middle of each nail. My aunt Lyra has this cool lightning tattoo on her ankle. She says it symbolizes power and strength."

"Can we have purple lightning?" Clover asked.

"Why not?" Anna set to work, painting everybody's nails green and then adding the lightning. She was on Mia's last nail when Clover changed the music and put on a Broadway show tunes playlist.

"Oh, I love this one!" Anna finished her last stroke and jumped up to sing "Defying Gravity," using the purple nail polish jar as a short, stubby microphone. Mia and Clover joined in, and half a verse later, they were all dancing around the room, waving their hands, belting out that part about not playing by anybody else's rules.

"Careful!" Anna shouted when Clover waved her not-quite-dry nails too close to Mia's bedpost. "Don't smudge them!"

"Sorry, but I love this part." Clover jumped up on Mia's bed, carefully picked up Neptune, and sang to him. "Just this stingray and I . . . defyyyyyy . . . ing gravity . . ."

Mia and Anna jumped up, too, for the big finish.

"Wow!" Mia's door had been open, and now Mom was looking in, laughing. "That was quite a trio!"

"We're the Three Entrepreneurial Musketeers," Mia said, hopping down from the bed.

"We just do show tunes as a side gig," Clover added, and they all laughed.

Mom looked at Mia. "I love how much fun you're having with this. I have to run to the store. Need anything?"

"Nope." But seeing Mom's phone in her hand reminded Mia that she didn't know what was going on with Fiona. All of a sudden, her stomach tied itself in a knot. She turned to Anna and Clover. "I'll be right back."

She followed Mom downstairs. "Did you talk to Aunt Abby?"

Mom nodded. "Fiona's not going to Tumblers."

Mia hadn't realized she was holding her breath, but now she let it out in a rush, and her eyes filled with tears.

"It's okay, honey." Mom wrapped her in a hug. "I told Aunt Abby what you told me, and first off, she wanted to know if you're all right. I told her you are, but that I sure wouldn't be comfortable sending a kid there. So she called the other gym, and there were still openings. Fiona's going there instead."

Mia took a shuddery breath and waited for her stomach to unknot, but it didn't. "What about all the other girls? Did you talk to Coach Carrie?"

"I left a message," Mom said. "I'm sure she'll call back." She reached out and tipped up Mia's chin to look into her eyes. "Are you doing okay?"

Mia wiped her teary cheeks with her sleeve and nodded. She was. Mostly. "I mean, I'm excited for tomorrow. We've been having so much fun getting ready."

Mom smiled. "I noticed that. You were channeling Idina Menzel up there."

Mia nodded. "So mostly I'm okay. But once in a while, I think about what happened, and then I feel icky all over again."

Mom gave a sad nod. "I think that's natural. If you want, we can go see somebody who's an expert at helping people through things like this."

"There are experts in this?" It made Mia sad to know

there were enough Phils out there that there had to be experts in helping the people they hurt. "I don't know if I want to do that right now. But maybe later?"

"Anytime. You can come to me anytime, too. You've been so strong, Mia. And so brave."

Mia looked down at the purple lightning bolts on her fingernails. She'd never thought of herself that way. Not really. Not even back when she was jumping off those rocks. She'd just done that because she didn't know enough to be scared. But now, she realized, she could know things and be brave anyway. That was something.

"Mia?" Clover poked her head into the kitchen. "I don't mean to interrupt, but didn't you want to go see your gram out at the farm?"

Mia looked at the microwave clock. It was already four thirty. "Oh my gosh, yes. Thanks." She gave her mom a quick, fierce hug and whispered "I love you" in her ear. Mom left for the store, and Mia, Anna, and Clover went upstairs to get everything they needed.

Then they put on their helmets, packed up their spying moose, and biked out to the industrial park. It was time to put their double-agent moose to work.

CHAPTER 22

And the Winner Is . . .

Mr. Jacobson's car wasn't in the parking lot when they got there, so they went to see if Gram needed help with the crickets. As soon as they walked in, Syd made a beeline for Mia. Then she spotted Anna, stopped, and burst out barking.

Anna stepped back, but Clover said, "Don't worry. She used to hate me, too." Syd had already stopped barking, so Clover bent to love her up. "Remember that, oh, fierce one?" she said as Syd flopped over for a belly rub.

"Hello, ladies!" Gram said, coming out of the office. "Are you here to help out?"

"Sure!" Mia said.

"Perfect. Daniel got called in for his other job and didn't get to finish changing the waters if you want to do that."

"Wait, what?" Mia looked at Gram. "Daniel got another job?"

Gram nodded. "He didn't want to say anything, but he told me last week that he was going to do some work at the college on the side. In case I need to cut back his hours." Gram sighed. "I hope it doesn't come to that, but I can't blame him for having a backup plan."

"That makes sense." Mia was relieved to know Daniel's secret phone calls were really just about not hurting Gram's feelings. "And we can definitely help you."

"Great. I have a meeting soon and was in a bit of a pinch." Gram shook her head. "I tried to call Bob Jacobson because he said he could always help out, but he's off on a business trip."

Mia felt half-disappointed and half-relieved that she wouldn't have to go through with the moose-swapping plan today. "How long will he be gone?"

"Not long," Gram said. "His secretary said he had to run up to Quebec for something, but he'll be back by one or two tomorrow afternoon."

"Quebec?" Mia's heart sped up before she even understood why. But then the audio from the moose's memory card played back in her head.

That virus apparently gets into everything. She says a farm in Quebec just had it wipe out their whole population . . .

"Yes," Gram said, and gave Mia a funny look. "Got something against Quebec?"

"No." Mia forced herself to smile. She turned to Clover and Anna, who were giving her weird looks, too. They must not have made the connection. And Mia couldn't say anything about it. Not in front of the moose.

Her head was spinning as they washed the water dishes and gave the crickets food. Quebec was a big province, so maybe it was nothing. But what if Mr. Jacobson was visiting that cricket farm with the awful virus? What if he brought it back somehow and infected Gram's farm?

"You okay?" Clover asked as she blew at some crickets to make them move out of their food dish. "You got all quiet."

"I'm fine," Mia said. But then she shook her head and pointed at the moose, sticking out of her backpack in the corner. She hadn't wanted to leave it in the lobby where Gram might say something.

"I have to go to the bathroom," Clover said. "Can you show me where it is?"

"I have to go, too," Anna said, and followed them. "Mia, what's going on?" she whispered as soon as they closed the door.

"Mr. Jacobson is in *Quebec*." Mia reminded them about the infected cricket farm.

Clover gasped. "When did she say he's coming back?"

"One or two tomorrow afternoon."

"Okay . . ." Clover leaned against the sink and stared up at the ceiling, thinking. "We can still do the competition. Then we'll come straight here to make sure everything is all right, and we'll swap out the moose then." She looked at Mia. "Should we tell your gram about this?"

Mia shook her head. Gram had so much to worry about already. And also, Gram loved Mr. Jacobson. Everybody did. He had that friendly Phil thing going. Gram might believe him if he made up some stupid excuse about the listening device and said it was to record parents' voices for little kids or something.

No. They needed to nail him. They needed proof.

"Let's see what happens tomorrow," Mia said. "As long as the farm is okay for now, I think it'll be best to wait until we have real evidence."

"We'll have that as soon as we get the moose swapped out," Anna said.

Clover nodded, and they went back to the warehouse to finish their cricket work. Then Mia collected the moose, and they rode home. Mom made chili, and they ate upstairs while they watched movies and sang more Broadway songs to Neptune.

"Don't stay up too late, girls," Mom said when she checked in at ten.

She didn't have to worry. After a long day of bike riding and swimming and sleuthing, none of them kept their eyes open another ten minutes.

Vermont Launch Junior was happening in the ballroom of a fancy downtown hotel. Mia's parents dropped them off, and the plan was for Clover's mom to bring them to the cricket farm to help Gram after the competition. That's what Mia told her parents, even though she'd really be on a mission to plant the spy moose in Mr. Jacobson's office. Anna had to stop in at her cousin's birthday party after the competition, but she'd come out to join them as soon as she could get away.

"Do you have the laptop?" Clover asked as she carried the poster board inside.

"Yep—also the banner and cricket samples," Mia said.

"I've got the robot." Anna was lugging a huge box because the robot had to be packed in foam so its parts didn't get jostled and messed up on the car ride. Robots were more fragile than molting crickets, apparently.

Before the presentation, there was an hour-long exhibition where the public could look at projects and talk with entrepreneurs. At ten, the first of the ten teams would give their talk while the judges sat in a row, *Deal with the Sharks*–style, taking notes and asking questions. Mia,

Clover, and Anna were scheduled second to last. Then there would be a fifteen-minute break before awards. After that, they'd race out the door to the cricket farm.

"I hope this really ends by noon," Mia said as she poured barbecue crickets into sample cups. "We have to get back before—"

"Shh!" Anna pointed to the duffel bag under their table. Mia was really looking forward to ditching that moose.

"It'll be okay," Clover said as the doors opened and people streamed into the ballroom. "Now let's do this thing."

For an hour, they gave out cricket samples, took Chirp Challenge photos, and answered questions about eating crickets as food.

"Yes, they really are a healthy protein."

"No, these crickets didn't come from a field somewhere."

"Sure, the legs get stuck in your teeth sometimes, but you get used to that."

At ten o'clock, the presentations started. The first team had set up a homework-helpers hotline for their school. Aidan was up next with Cookies for a Cause, and the judges seemed to love him. Some were surprised when he mentioned he had a chocolate *chirp* cookie made with cricket flour on his list of fund-raiser options, but Aidan just smiled and said, "Don't worry. You'll hear more about that soon."

Dylan and Julia were up next. Dylan left his skateboard at his seat and held the jewelry display board while Julia talked about how eco-friendly their earrings were. She lifted one of her braids so the judges could see hers better. When they were done, Eli and Nick came running out in team uniforms, kicking soccer balls, and then stopped mid-kick and looked around. "Aw, rats!" Eli said. "I was hoping there'd be a game here today." Mia had to admit it was a funny way to get attention for KicksFinder. As obnoxious as Eli could be, she envied his confidence. He and his dimples just walked around, sure that everyone would love them wherever they went. And most people did.

They loved Clover, too. She joined Eli and Nick onstage to talk about her work with the coding, and the judges seemed impressed.

Two hockey players came out after them—also in uniform—to pitch their Hockey-Fresh equipment bags, which had built-in air fresheners. One of the judges sniffed the bag and said it smelled like a mix of sweat and lilacs, which made Mia think that team wouldn't be getting a whole lot of points.

The next entrepreneur was a high school junior who was marketing Cool Patch, for when you rip your jeans, with a new kind of adhesive she'd invented. She'd done all the chemistry for it and had a patent pending and everything.

Then came a girl who made her own lemonade, with honey from bees she raised herself, and another girl who created an app called FishDetector for finding the best fishing spots. Mia only listened to half her pitch because she was getting nervous.

And then it was their turn.

"And now we have the Green Mountain Cricket Farm team," the announcer said.

Mia took a deep breath and forced herself to follow Clover and Anna onto the stage. She had to start the pitch.

"Good morning!" she said, and then hesitated. One judge gave her an encouraging smile. Mia stared back at her. The judges sat facing away from the audience, so Mia hadn't seen her face until now. It was Anne Marie Spangler from Five Dogs Apparel. From the event at the college where Mia had talked with her afterward and told her— Why had she told a stranger that? And what was Anne Marie doing here?

Actually, Mia knew what she was doing. She was judging the contest with the other businesspeople, and they were all waiting for Mia to talk. It was good she'd practiced so much, because now the words tumbled out without her thinking. "What if I told you that eating insects could provide a healthier lifestyle for your family and save the planet at the same time?" Clover held the poster board while Mia shared all the crickets' promises about protein and sustainability. "We're not launching a new cricket farm," she said, "but we've put together a marketing, automation, and expansion plan for the one my grandmother runs right here in Vermont. My colleagues, Clover and Anna, will tell you more about that."

There. Mia stepped back while Clover talked about the challenges of getting people to eat insects and ideas for viral marketing. She shared the mayor's social media post. "We believe that by targeting key influencers like this, we can grow. But we need to be more efficient, and Anna has a plan for that."

Anna brought her robot to the front of the stage, explained how long it takes to harvest crickets by hand, and ran a perfect demonstration of her robot harvester. Then Mia wrapped up by talking about their open house the next day and invited everyone—judges and audience alike—to join Gram at the farm to see for themselves. "And finally, now that you've heard our pitch . . ." Mia held up a tub of roasted crickets and gave it a shake, just like Gram had when she greeted them that day at the farm. "Who would like to try a crispy barbecue cricket or two?"

Every judge's hand went up, and most of the audience raised their hands, too. Mia hadn't planned on that, so Clover ran to the display table for more samples.

"Thanks so much for the chance to share our project," Mia said. She hadn't looked at Anne Marie the whole time, but she did now, and Anne Marie gave her a little nod.

Then Mia went back to her seat and collapsed. Clover and Anna grabbed her hands, one on each side, and squeezed, as Quan and Bella went up to give the last presentation of the day.

"We did it!" Clover whispered. "Don't you think it went great? I think we have a chance at placing."

Mia thought so, too. But she didn't really understand how this whole thing worked. Gymnastics had been easier to figure out. You lost a certain number of points for falling off the beam or missing a catch on the uneven bars, and by the time you landed, you had a pretty good idea what your score would be. Who knew what these judges were looking for? Mia *felt* like it had gone well, but she was afraid to hope and then feel dumb about it, so she put a finger to her lips and pointed at the stage, where Quan was talking about the popularity of food trucks.

When they finished, the judges thanked everyone and promised to come back in fifteen minutes to announce winners. Mia, Clover, and Anna went to their table to clean up. The robot had to be packed up in foam again, so Anna worked on that while Mia and Clover tossed out empty sample cups. There weren't any crickets left, which Mia thought was a good sign.

"I hope they decide fast." She looked up at the clock on

the wall. It was ten after twelve. "Maybe we should go. What if this takes a while?"

"We can't leave. You were amazing, Mia. We rocked this." Clover turned to Mia, grabbed her hand, and reached out to take Anna's, too.

Mia looked down at their sparkly green fingernails with the purple lightning. It was only nail polish, but Mia swore it had worked some kind of magic, giving her the strength to finish her talk while she was up onstage. Or maybe that was just because her friends were there beside her.

"Look!" Anna pointed. "They're already back."

Everyone went to their seats while the judges filed in. Mia looked at the clock. By the time the judges got settled, it was quarter after twelve. What if Mr. Jacobson had come back from Quebec early?

Clover's phone buzzed, and she looked down. "My mom's here, so we can head out as soon as this is done."

One of the judges stepped up to the podium. "First, I'd like to congratulate all of you," he said. "Our job wasn't easy, but we do have winners to announce. First, two honorable mentions: Cookies for a Cause and Lucy's Honey-Lime Lemonade!"

"Go, Aidan!" Mia clapped as he and the bee girl went up to get certificates.

"Our third place honor goes to . . ."

Mia's heart could have burst out of her chest. Could they really have placed?

". . . the Bao Bus!"

"Woo-hoo!" Clover shouted as Quan and Bella collected their trophy.

Clover's eyes were all big and excited. She leaned over to Mia and whispered, "I have a very good feeling about this."

"In second place . . . ," the judge announced, "KicksFinder!"

Figures, Mia thought. But she clapped as Eli and Nick went up to get their trophy. Clover joined them but hurried back to Mia and Anna. "This is it."

Mia sucked in her breath and looked up at the ceiling as the applause died down. She'd been afraid to hope, but now, that hope was a big bubble in her chest that felt as if it might lift her right off the ground and up to the fancy hotel chandelier.

"And now, the first-place winner of this year's Vermont Launch Junior is . . ." He paused and looked out over the audience before he looked back down at his paper. "Cool Patch!"

Mia's hope deflated. She forced herself to clap for the chemistry girl. The newspaper reporters—the ones who wouldn't be doing stories on Gram's cricket farm now—gathered around her, and everybody in the audience got up to leave.

"Sorry," Clover said. "I really thought we had a chance." She gave Mia and Anna half-hearted fist bumps.

"Me too," said Anna.

"You two were amazing," Mia said. "Thank you so much for everything." She smiled, but it felt like somebody had stepped all over her heart with muddy boots.

Then she looked at the clock and felt even worse. It was already twelve thirty. "Clover, we need to go!"

They hugged Anna, who was leaving with her parents for the birthday party, and then Clover turned to Mia. "Go get the moose, okay? I'll grab our poster and stuff."

Mia was on her way to pick up her duffel bag full of moose when she felt a hand on her shoulder.

"Mia?" It was Anne Marie Spangler, with a clipboard full of notes in her hand. Another lady was standing next to her. "Could we speak with you for a minute?"

CHAPTER 23

Like a Kung Fu Mantis

"Do you know what an angel investor is?"

Mia nodded. Then she said, "Kind of," because really, she only remembered Daniel saying that Gram needed to find some to keep her business going.

"Angel investors provide funding for start-ups in exchange for partial ownership." Anne Marie gestured to the other woman. "Miranda and I are part of a group of local investors with a focus on supporting women entrepreneurs. We were incredibly impressed with your project, and we'd like to talk about the possibility of investing in your grandmother's farm."

"Really?" Mia said. "We didn't even get an honorable mention."

"That's true," Anne Marie said, "because the competition was set up with a specific rubric and point structure. But when it comes to real-world investing, we look at more than that."

"So you want to give my grandmother money? And own part of her farm?"

"Maybe. If she's open to that idea." Anne Marie held out a business card. "Would you ask her to contact me if she'd like to talk?"

Mia looked at the card but didn't take it right away. Had they really done such a good job that they'd convinced her to invest in Gram's farm? Or was this about something else? *It shouldn't matter,* Mia thought. She should give Gram the card and be glad it was happening at all. But she had to know. "Are you doing this because . . . because of what I told you after your presentation?"

Anne Marie looked at her friend and said, "Can you give us just a minute?" Miranda nodded and went to talk with the other judges.

"Mia," Anne Marie said. "I'm glad you talked to me about what happened. And I hope you've found someone else to talk with, too. Someone you know well and trust."

Mia nodded. "I told my mom yesterday."

Anne Marie raised her eyebrows. "How did that go?"

"It was good," Mia said. "Really good. I mean, it was hard, too. But I'm glad I told her."

"Me too," Anne Marie said. "But I want you to know that has nothing to do with why I'm interested in this project." She turned her clipboard so Mia could see. It was covered with notes from her presentation—everything from the farm's expansion possibilities to Clover's social media campaign and Anna's harvesting robot. Anne Marie had scribbled other little notes, too.

Expected growth potential?

Other possibilities for automation?

"I'm a businesswoman, Mia. A very successful one. And I didn't get here by investing in things because I felt sorry for people or because I just like them. I'm successful because I'm smart, and I know a promising opportunity when I see it. You showed me one today." She held out the business card again. "We believe in your project. We can help with the business plan and provide the funding your grandmother needs to make this work. We believe it's essential that women support other women. But make no mistake, we're doing this because we want to make money. And we think your grandmother can."

This time, Mia took the card. "Thank you."

"Mia, you ready?" Clover was standing there with the poster board.

"Oh!" Mia had forgotten why she was in a hurry. "I have to go. But thanks! Again!" She and Clover hurried out to the car. Mia put her duffel bag with the moose in the trunk, and then the girls piled in the back seat, where Mia told Clover everything Anne Marie had said.

"That's amazing!" Clover said.

"I can't wait to tell Gram!" Mia was clutching the business card so tight it was getting sweaty. She tucked it in her back pocket so it wouldn't be in shreds by the time they got to the farm. "I just hope everything's still okay," she whispered to Clover. It was ten minutes to one now. If they didn't beat Mr. Jacobson back, there might not *be* a farm to invest in.

Clover's mom had to stop for gas, which made Mia want to scream, but she told herself that waiting another three minutes was better than running out of gas.

Finally, they pulled into the cricket farm parking lot, and Clover's mom dropped them off. "His car's not here," Mia said as they headed for the door of the farm. A wave of relief rushed over her. Now they could go inside and talk to Gram about the angel investors and figure out how they were going to—

"Here he comes," Clover said.

Mia froze as Mr. Jacobson pulled into his parking spot. Her duffel bag full of moose felt heavy on her shoulder. She was going to have to do this.

Mr. Jacobson didn't seem to see them. He and another man Mia hadn't seen before got out of the car. Mr. Jacobson opened the back hatch and pulled out a big plastic bin. Mia's heart raced. "We can't let him go inside with that!"

"How are we going to stop him?" Clover whispered. "We don't even know if that's—"

"But it might be! And if it is, there's nothing we can do once it's inside." None of it would matter. Not their business plan or the open house tomorrow or Anne Marie and Miranda's investment. If that virus got into the farm, it was over.

Mr. Jacobson and the other man started for the back door of the warehouse. Mia ran around in front of them.

"Hi, Mr. Jacobson!" she said. "Can I help you carry that?"

"No thanks!" he said. "Just some supplies we need to upgrade the sewing machines. My new employee, Mitch, is an expert with machines. This is his first day in town, and we need to get going so I can show him around."

"Can I see?" Mia was desperate. "I like sewing."

He laughed. "Nothing interesting." He started to step around her.

"Wait!" Clover ran up to them. "Can we interview you for our camp project? We have to talk to successful entrepreneurs."

"I'd be happy to do that," he said, "but it'll have to wait."

He looked at Mia, still standing in his way. "We need to get going now, I'm afraid."

"What's in that box?" Mia blurted out, louder this time.

Mr. Jacobson's eyes narrowed. He heard Mia's question as a challenge, and that was fine. That's how she'd meant it.

Her heart was thumping so wildly, she was sure he could hear, but she didn't move. She thought about Clover facing down that awful swimsuit man on the beach, and Anne Marie firing her old boss, and her mom putting up with so much at her first law-firm job. And Gram. Mia thought about Gram, and she stayed put.

"Enough of this nonsense, girls." He started to go around Mia, but his keys slid off the top of the bin. When he put it down to pick them up, Mia didn't even think. She yanked the lid off the box. It was full of dead crickets.

The other man—Mitch—snatched the lid from her and shoved it back onto the bin. "You must have grabbed the wrong box," he told Mr. Jacobson. His voice sounded familiar to Mia.

"Of course!" Mr. Jacobson turned to Mia. "These are crickets I bought from your grandmother."

Mia stared at him. "No you didn't!" She stood in front of him with her arms crossed. She was terrified, but more than that, she was angry. "You got those crickets from that farm in Quebec that got wiped out by the virus. And now you're trying to bring them here!"

"Virus? That's ridiculous." Mr. Jacobson's voice had a shaky edge to it. "I've done nothing but support your grandmother ever since she got here."

"By spying on her? And on us?" Mia unzipped her duffel bag and yanked out the moose. "We found the bug in your stupid moose's ear."

Just then, the cricket-farm door opened, and Syd came racing out, wagging her tail. Mia waited for her to bark at the stranger. But Syd didn't bark at Mitch. She ran up to him, flopped down on his foot, and rolled over for a belly rub.

Now Mia knew where she'd heard that voice.

"This isn't your first day here at all!" she said. "You helped him bring in the fruit flies! And I bet you messed with Gram's thermostat and freezer, too!"

Mr. Jacobson's face was so red Mia thought he might burst into flames. He grabbed the moose out of her hands and shoved her backward so hard she stumbled over the curb and fell.

"Hey!" Clover ran to help Mia up. Mr. Jacobson picked up his bin, whirled around, and hurried to his car.

Mia was shaking. Her hands were scraped from the sidewalk, but she couldn't think about what was safe or what was smart. She wanted him to know he hadn't won. She put her hands on her hips and stood up as tall as she could, kung fu mantis–style. "We know what you did!"

"Congratulations, Nancy Drew." He shoved the box and the moose into his trunk. "But if you don't have the moose, you don't have the evidence." He looked at Mia over his shoulder. "And you know what? I never even needed these infected crickets because your grandmother's just a delusional old lady who's going to run her little business into the ground all by herself, and then I'll be able to take over her lease and expand my warehouse. But thanks for the entertainment." He slammed the hatch. Then both men got into the car, and they peeled out of the parking lot.

Mia sat on the curb and tried to catch her breath. Syd waddled up and licked her elbow.

"I don't even know what's going on anymore. I figured he was working with Mr. Potsworth, but now it sounds like it was all him, wanting more warehouse space." She shook her head. "I guess it doesn't really matter because he's right. Without the moose, we're kind of done."

"But we're witnesses," Clover said.

"We're kids," Mia said. "And he's a successful business owner." She sighed. "I should have held on to the moose."

"At least he's gone," Clover said, pulling Mia to her feet. "We need to tell your grandmother about all this now, don't you think?"

Mia nodded and followed Clover inside.

"Hey, girls!" Gram said. "How was your competition?"

"Good," Mia said. She didn't know where to start. "But we have to talk to you about something else."

They told her everything. Mia thought Gram would freak out, but she just listened. Her eyes looked so mad Mia thought they might burn a hole through the wall. When they finished, Gram nodded sharply. "All right. At least we know what we're up against now."

"Are you going to call the police?" Mia asked.

"I will," Gram said, "but I'm afraid they won't have much to work with."

"Can't they go to his house and search it?" Clover asked.

"Not without a warrant." Mia had picked up enough law from Mom to know that.

"They'd need actual evidence for that," Gram added.

"And we lost the evidence with the moose," Mia said.

"No you didn't!"

Anna came racing into the room with her laptop under one arm.

"I thought you had a birthday party," Clover said.

"I did!" Anna paused to catch her breath. "But we had to stop home first, and while my mom was getting ready to go, I pulled up the moose audio feed on my laptop."

"You pulled up what?" Mia said.

"The audio feed from your moose." When Mia and Clover still looked confused, she said, "I guess I never finished telling you. When I took the moose home that night to turn it into a double agent, I set it up to transmit. It was kind of a pain because I needed a SIM card, and you have to be eighteen for that, so Prima had to get it for me. Anyway, she helped me connect the microphone to a microcontroller, and that was connected to the Internet via the SIM card to send audio back to my laptop in real time."

"What does that mean, like, in English?" Clover asked.

"It means I have every word of what just happened, recorded right here." Anna put the laptop down on the lobby table, opened it up, and tapped at the keys. Mr. Jacobson's voice came out of the speakers.

"If you don't have the moose, you don't have the evidence." His voice was clear as could be. *"And you know what? I never even needed these infected crickets because your grandmother's just a delusional old lady who's going to run her little business into the ground all by herself, and then I'll be able to take over her lease and expand my warehouse."*

"Thanks for the confession, jerk!" Clover said.

"Delusional old lady? Run my *little business* into the ground myself . . ." Gram's lips were pressed together tight. She let out a sharp breath. Then she shook her head as if to shake off Mr. Jacobson and his crummy, jerky words. "I'm going to call the police now," she said. "And then I want to hear all about your competition because we never got to that."

After Gram went to her office, Mia turned to Anna. "You are the absolute best," she said. "You are the techno-geek of all techno-geeks."

"Thanks," Anna said. "I gotta go because everybody's waiting. I made Dad stop here before the party." She handed Mia a flash drive. "Here's a copy of the conversation. I'll make another backup just in case. Let me know if the police need anything else."

When Gram returned, Mia and Clover told her all about the business plan they'd developed for the cricket farm. They showed her their poster board and answered questions about Anna's cricket harvesting robot. Then Mia handed her the business card and told her what Anne Marie Spangler had said. Gram stared at it, and her eyes filled with tears.

Gram never ever cried. But her voice broke when she turned to Mia. "You know what? I'd thought about pitching to this investors group at one of their meetings, but I decided they wouldn't want to hear from an old lady like me." She looked at Mia. "You were braver than that. And

I'm so glad." She hugged Mia and Clover and said, "Are you girls hungry?"

"Starving, actually," Mia said. They'd missed lunch.

"Let's order a pizza and get to work," Gram said. "The police are on their way. And in the meantime, we've got an open house to prepare."

CHAPTER 24

Lake Monster Security and Punk-Rock Crickets

Gram had set up a meeting with Anne Marie for Sunday afternoon, so she pretty much turned the public part of the open house over to Mia, Clover, and Anna.

Clover set up their Chirp Challenge banner at the sample table. She and Mia made copies of different recipes to give away—chocolate chirp cookies and cricket tacos and apple-kale-cricket smoothies. They had a display of local restaurants and shops that were using Green Mountain crickets as ingredients, and they all had samples, too. There were cricket crispies from the Chocolate Shoppe, and later on, Mom was bringing Thai cricket pizza from Mazzella's and a cooler full of Creepy Coconut Cricket Crunch ice cream from Tom and Harry's.

Dad was there, helping out, too. Mia had asked Mom if she'd talk to him about the Phil thing so Mia didn't have to go through the whole story again. Dad wasn't great at talking about stuff like that, but first thing this morning, he'd given Mia a hug and said, "I love you, and I'm so proud of you." Now he was doing everything he could to make Mia laugh, and she was grateful for that, too. Gram had assigned Dad to blow up balloons. He kept taking big gulps of helium and saying, "Hi! I'm Jiminy Cricket, and I want to be your healthy protein source!" in his silly, high helium voice.

"You can't do that once real people get here," Mia said. "Nobody wants to eat Jiminy."

Anna brought her harvesting robot to demonstrate and set that up on another table to shake cricket condos. "It's too bad we can't do an actual harvest," she said, "but at least people will get the idea."

"Where's Daniel?" Clover asked. "He's going to love this!"

"He's been assigned security duty. With his entire team." Mia pointed out the window. She'd noticed them when Mom dropped her off. Daniel and a bunch of Lake Monsters players were lurking in the trees around the warehouse. She couldn't believe she'd thought he might be behind the sabotage. "Gram says they're going to keep watch all day, just in case."

No one had seen Mr. Jacobson or heard from the police since last night, but at nine thirty, half an hour before the open house started, a detective arrived. She went into Gram's office and closed the door. Ten minutes later, they came out. Gram said goodbye and sent the detective off with a tub of barbecue crickets and a sample of protein powder.

"Well, we can tell Daniel to call off the patrol outside," she announced. "They arrested Bob Jacobson this morning."

"Yes!" Mia pumped her fist in the air. "Did they find those awful crickets?"

Gram nodded. "After they listened to the recordings, they went to Bob's house and set up surveillance. Late last night, they saw him leave with a bin and followed him to a big trash bin behind the hospital. They recovered the dead crickets, and when they confronted him at his house later, he confessed."

"So it was just him? He wasn't working with Mr. Potsworth?"

Gram shook her head. "Chet Potsworth was pretty pushy about asking me to sell, but I was wrong about him being behind the sabotage. He wasn't involved in any of it. I feel a little bad about that."

"Yeah." Mia felt a little bad about breaking into his food-processing plant, too, but nobody needed to know about that today.

"So . . ." Gram looked at her watch. "How are we doing here?"

"We're all set with samples," Mia said. "We're just waiting for—"

"Cricket pizza's here!" Mom came through the door with five steaming boxes. "Where do you want these?"

"Right here." Mia pointed to the display table. "Where's the ice cream?"

"In my trunk," Mom said, and Dad went out to help her bring it in.

While they dealt with the ice cream, Mia and Clover set up a craft table for little kids. They had crayons and coloring pages and pipe cleaners, so kids could make cricket antennae to wear for their Chirp Challenge selfies.

Clover made a wild orange, pink, and green set of antennae and put it on. "How do I look?"

"Like a punk-rock cricket." Mia laughed and took a picture with her phone. She looked around the lobby. It was ten minutes to ten, and they were ready. The samples were waiting. Clover had sent out press releases to all the TV stations and newspapers. Now people just had to show up.

"Mia, can you come out to the car with me for a second?" Mom called from across the room. "I have more supplies to bring in."

"Sure." Mia followed Mom to the car and waited for her to open the trunk.

Instead, Mom leaned against the door and looked at Mia. "I was a little late with the ice cream because I was on the phone with Coach Carrie."

"You were?" Mia's heart sped up. "What did she say?"

"She'd just gotten a phone call from another parent."

"Oh no." Mia's eyes filled with tears. "No. Who? I should have said something sooner. I'm so sorry."

"No." Mom put a hand on Mia's shoulder. "It's okay. It's not like that. He didn't seriously hurt anyone. Not that we know of. But there was another girl who felt uncomfortable around him, and when her mom talked with her, she showed her text messages he'd sent that were . . . wrong. Not the kinds of messages any adult should send a kid. Based on that and what you were brave enough to share, the gym has suspended him, and they've opened a wider investigation. With the police."

Mia's head was spinning. "So what does that mean?"

"They'll interview lots of people. Everyone he's had contact with, including at the gym where he worked before. And they'll make sure that what happened to you doesn't happen to anyone else."

Mia took a deep breath.

"This is exactly what should be happening, Mia. You did a really good thing."

Mia nodded. "Thanks." She wiped the tear that had escaped down her cheek. "I still think about it a bunch." She paused. "I might want to talk to somebody else, too. One of those expert people you talked about."

Mom nodded. "We can do that anytime."

"Not yet," Mia said. "But maybe when everything quiets down."

"Anytime," Mom said again, and hugged her.

Then a car pulled into the parking lot, and a dad and three kids got out. They pointed to Gram's open-house sign and headed for the door as two more cars and a mini-van pulled in.

"Wow," Mia said. "People are actually showing up for this."

Mom smiled. "Your grandmother is so proud of you," she said. "So are we." She pulled Mia into one more quick, tight hug. "We can talk more later if you want. But right now, you should get in there and serve some crickets."

CHAPTER 25

Crickets, Warriors, and Taking Things Back

The open house was a whirlwind. Everybody from Launch Camp came. Quan and Bella took a zillion Chirp Challenge selfies. Eli went straight over to Anna, and Mia was about to go rescue her when she heard Eli say, "This robot is the coolest thing to come out of Launch Camp."

"Thanks." Anna looked like she was bracing for him to start bugging her about going for ice cream again, but Eli looked down. "Listen, I'm . . . really sorry about how I acted when we were working together. After the competition yesterday, my mom asked why you weren't on our team anymore, and when I told her, she let me have it."

"Good," Anna said, adjusting her robot arm.

"I know. I do now, anyway, and I just . . . I wanted to

say sorry." He shuffled away to the balloons, where Nick was talking like a chipmunk. Pretty soon, they were both squeaking and laughing.

"You think he meant that apology?" Mia asked.

"Seemed like it." Anna shrugged. "We'll see how he acts when we get back to school." She looked up. "Hey, there's the honey-lime-lemonade girl!"

Mia waved and then recognized a bunch of other Vermont Launch kids, along with some people from the audience. Anne Marie and Miranda were there, too, for their meeting with Gram, and then they volunteered to help hand out balloons.

Since Daniel's Lake Monster buddies didn't need to patrol outside anymore, they came in and posed for selfies with everybody. They also got to share the fun news that the Lake Monsters would soon be serving roasted crickets at the ballpark concession stand during games.

A bunch of kids from Warrior Camp came before their extra Sunday Fun-Day session that started at noon. Mia and Clover were hoping to catch the tail end of that if the open house ended on time.

Chet Potsworth from the food-processing plant showed up, too. When he walked over to talk with Gram, Mia switched from the sample table to the craft center so she could listen.

"I understand now that you're not interested in selling,"

he said, "but I heard this week that you might be taking on some investors, and I'd really like to be considered."

"We can talk about that," Gram said. "Let's set up a meeting next week."

The open house ran through lunch. Mia and Clover scarfed down Thai cricket pizza slices while they were attaching pipe cleaner antennae to headbands.

"Got a slice for me?" someone asked.

"Mayor Obasanjo!" Clover jumped to her feet.

Mia stood up and shook the mayor's hand. "Thanks for sharing that picture from the farmers market. You have no idea how much that helped us."

"That's great to hear," the mayor said, arranging her cricket antennae. "I think my new headgear definitely calls for another selfie. You want to be in it, too?"

Mia and Clover called Anna over, and they all put on antennae and posed with the mayor.

"I love to see local businesses thriving," Mayor Obasanjo said. "Congratulations on this terrific turnout."

By the time the mayor bought some protein powder and left, it was five minutes to two, and the crowd was starting to thin.

"How did the Chirp Challenge go today?" Mom asked. For someone who didn't really approve of Gram's cricket farm, she'd been a huge help. She was even wearing a pair of antennae.

"Great! It's not too late, you know . . ." Mia grinned and held up a cup of roasted crickets.

"What's this?" Gram came rushing over. "Somebody call the newspapers! Is my daughter-in-law finally going to eat a cricket?"

Mia looked at Mom and raised her eyebrows. "You should at least try one."

Mom sighed. Then she smiled and picked up a single cricket between two fingers.

"Wait! Let me get a picture!" Clover grabbed her phone and positioned Mom under the Chirp Challenge banner. "Okay, go ahead."

Mom looked from Mia to Gram. "I'm only doing this because I admire both of you so much. Here goes . . ." She posed for Clover's picture, then dropped the cricket into her mouth, chewed quickly, and swallowed. "Okay," she said. "That could have been worse."

"That's our best endorsement yet," Gram said, laughing, and went to let Syd out of the office. Syd had been banished so she wouldn't launch a waddle-bark attack on the guests. Poor dog. She'd have to figure out someday that not all strangers were awful and not everybody who gave you a pat on the head was okay.

Mia took a break from cleaning the craft table to rub Syd's belly while Clover rolled up the banner. Then they said goodbye to Anna, packed away the few cricket samples that people hadn't scarfed down, and finished the last of the pizza and half-melted Creepy Coconut Cricket Crunch ice cream.

"We can't let it go to waste," Clover said, crunching on a chocolate-covered cricket.

"That would be awful," Mia agreed. "Although we won't be able to move at Sunday Fun-Day if we finish all this."

"Oh!" Clover looked at the clock. "I forgot about that, but I really want to go."

"We'll still have half an hour if we leave now," Mia said. "Here, Syd!" She put her paper plate down and let Syd gobble up what was left of her pizza crust. They grabbed their gym bags, changed in the farm bathroom, hugged Gram goodbye, and headed down the hall to the gym.

"Ten feet today." Clover reached out for a fist bump. "You're going to hit ten feet on that warped wall."

"Ten feet?" Mia said. "Nah. I'm going all the way to the top."

Mia didn't get to the top. And she didn't quite hit the ten-foot mark, either. But it didn't matter. She was close, and everybody cheered, and way too soon, it was time to go home.

"My mom's outside. Need a ride?" Clover asked as they headed down the hallway.

Mia shook her head. "I'm going to see if Gram needs more help." Both their phones dinged with a text then. It was Anna.

We should go swimming at that place again!

Clover looked at Mia. "You in?"

Mia nodded. "Want to meet there at four?"

"Perfect." Clover texted Anna back, then waved and bounded out to the parking lot.

Mia picked up her duffel bag and looked for her water bottle to have a drink. It wasn't there, so she headed back to camp to find it.

Maria and Joe had already locked the Warrior Camp gym, but through the window, Mia could see her water bottle next to the warped wall. She'd have to get it on Tuesday. As she was leaving, she stopped at the big window that looked into the gymnastics room. They had Sunday Fun-Day, too, but later in the day, so theirs was just getting started.

"Hey there!" That Jamie lady popped her head out the door. "That invitation to try out our program still stands. And it's Sunday Fun-Day, so you're welcome to join us for a while if you'd like. Your Warrior Camp paperwork covers you here, too, so it's fine if you want to pop in for a quick vault or turn on the bars."

Mia looked through the window. A tall, skinny girl was tumbling down the length of the mat. A boy was running toward the vault. Another girl was just jumping onto the bars. The balance beam was empty.

It was strange. Mia didn't miss gymnastics anymore. Not really. But something about that beam tugged at her. She hadn't given it up on purpose.

"Actually . . . is it okay if I try one thing? Just for a minute?"

"Absolutely." Jamie held open the door. "Let me know if you need anything, okay?" She ran off to talk with another coach by the mats.

Mia sat down and took off her sneakers and socks. Then she walked up to the beam. She ran a hand along the rough leather and felt her Warrior Camp calluses scratch against it. Her heart sped up, but she closed her eyes and breathed in slowly. Then out slowly.

And then she mounted the beam.

It still felt so familiar under her bare feet. She held out her arms and walked to the end.

She lifted on her toes and pivoted.

She walked back.

She waited for her stomach to drop. Waited for the panic she thought might come. But it didn't. She was just there.

Mia on the balance beam.

She leaned forward into an arabesque. She did a tuck jump and landed. She wobbled just a little. And then she found her balance.

Mia felt the muscles in her legs, strong and steady from Warrior Camp. She felt the cool, hard leather under her feet. Solid, and steady, and hers again. If she wanted it.

She didn't think she did. And that was okay. There were other things she wanted back, though.

Mia did a roundoff. And totally stuck the landing.

She found Jamie to say thanks. Then she went back to the farm, helped Gram feed the crickets, stopped home to change her clothes, and rode her bike to meet Clover and Anna.

"Mia!" they shouted as she climbed down to the beach. They were camped out on a towel with their water bottles, sharing an enormous bag of potato chips. "We haven't been in yet," Clover said. "We waited for you."

"Well, I'm here now!" Mia said. "And I'm melting." She pulled off the T-shirt and shorts she had on over her swimsuit. Then she climbed up onto the jumping rocks.

"Woo-hoo!" Clover shouted. "You go, girl!"

Mia had thought about it the whole bike ride there. She wanted her rocks back. She wanted the brightness of that blue sky like in the photo. All summer, she'd been hoping she might find her way back to that girl in the picture, but she'd been thinking about it all wrong. It wasn't about finding her way back. The rainbow swimsuit didn't fit anymore. She'd have to find her way forward.

Mia planted her feet on the warm rocks and stood up tall. She wasn't doing the kung fu mantis thing. She was just done being small. She had a new purple-and-blue two-piece. She loved the way it showed off her Warrior Camp muscles, and she wasn't ashamed of that.

It showed off her battle scars, too. Even though they'd faded with her summer tan, the scars on her arm would always be a part of her. That was fine, too. But nobody else got to say who she was going to be. Mia would decide that herself. She deserved that.

She deserved to speak up and swing on swings and spell out her name with sparklers if she wanted. And she deserved to jump off rocks with her friends.

They were chanting her name now. "Mia! Mia!"

Mia flashed them a peace sign and held it while Clover took a picture with her phone. Then she turned to the lake. A breeze lifted her hair and cooled her face. She looked out over the waves. The sky was just like it had been in the picture, that impossibly perfect blue.

Mia looked across the lake at the Adirondack Mountains, all purple and hazy in the afternoon light. She breathed in the sunshine. Then she took three quick steps, leaped from the rocks, and soared through the summer air.

AUTHOR'S NOTE

I learned a lot about entomophagy while I was writing this book. Thanks to Steve and Jen Swanson of Flourish Farm for the crash course in cricket farming, and to Steve Hood for talking me through the business aspects of running a start-up like Gram's farm. I'm also grateful to Gabe Mott of Aspire Food Group in Austin, for showing me around the company's cricket farm operation and talking with me about automation and cricket-farming setbacks. If you'd like to read more about entomophagy (and other thoughts on eating more sustainably), I recommend the book *Diet for a Changing Climate: Food for Thought* by Christy Mihaly and Sue Heavenrich (Lerner, 2018).

Mia and Clover's Warrior Camp was inspired by my visit to Vermont Ninja Warrior Training Center in Essex, Vermont. Thanks to Chris Tower, McKinley Pierce, Amir Malik, and all the young warriors who answered my questions and allowed me to sit in on their camp.

The parts of this story that deal with Mia's and Clover's experiences with harassment were inspired by stories in the news and my own experiences growing up, as well as those of many women I'm lucky enough to call friends. I have so much love and respect for the women who have shared stories with me over the years and endless gratitude for those who stood by me as I shared my own. You are all warriors, braver than you know.

When we were growing up, kids weren't always encouraged to speak up when something felt wrong. Thankfully, that has begun to change, but there is more work to do. It's my greatest hope that Mia's story will help move that conversation forward and that readers who see themselves in these pages will understand that they are not alone. Not by a long shot.

The world is full of caring, wonderful adults who work as coaches, clergy members, and scout leaders, and in many other roles, helping kids. But there are also a small number of adults who use those positions to gain kids' trust and harm them.

No matter how old you are, no one has the right to touch you in a way that makes you uncomfortable. It doesn't matter who that person is. You have a right to say "Please stop touching me" or "I don't want a hug. How about a high five or fist bump?" Anyone who truly has your best interests in mind will respect that. If you find yourself in a bad situation that you can't handle on your own, you can always find help. Talk to a family member, or a trusted teacher or counselor at your school. And never forget how brave you are, every day, whether you've found your voice yet or not.

AN INTERVIEW WITH THE AUTHOR: KATE MESSNER

As is characteristic of your middle-grade novels, *Chirp* touches upon challenging topics that young readers face in their day-to-day lives. Your characters model resilience and courage in their respective trials, as Mia does in *Chirp*. Why is it important to you to represent the strength of young people in your writing and why did you feel compelled to write about this topic in particular?

KM: As someone who taught young readers for more than fifteen years and still spends lots of time with them as I visit schools, I understand that there's often a disconnect between the happy-go-lucky stories some adults want children to read and the actual lives of kids. Real kids have to deal with real-world issues. They're affected by everything from the opioid epidemic to climate change, and sometimes, the adults in their lives let them down. Coming to terms with all of that is part of growing up, and when kids have models of resilience and hope in the books they read, they understand that they're not alone. When they meet characters who are bravely facing real-world struggles, they can borrow a little courage for their own lives, too.

You write realistic stories about tough realities that readers often encounter with an overlying spirit of hopefulness. What do you hope for the readers of *Chirp*?

KM: First and foremost, I hope that readers of *Chirp* will fall in love with Mia and her friends and be swept up in the fun summer mystery they're trying to unravel. But beyond that, I know that many readers of all ages will see elements of their own lives in Mia's story, and it's always my hope that those readers will feel less alone and maybe a little braver as a result of sharing a story that reflects their lives.

Finally, just how many crickets *were* tasted in the research process for this book?

KM: If you'd ever told me that being a cricket taster would be part of my life as a children's author, I'm not sure I would have believed it, but yes . . . I did a lot of exploration in the area of entomophagy, or eating insects as food. I visited cricket farms in Vermont and Texas and sampled everything from Thai cricket pizza to chocolate-covered-cricket ice cream to roasted crickets in half a dozen flavors. (Texas BBQ remains my favorite!) Cricket flour is another product that's gaining popularity, since it can be used to replace some of the carbs in baked goods with a little boost of cricket protein. The trick to baking with cricket flour seems to be replacing no more than twenty percent of a recipe's flour with cricket flour. Any more than that tends to mess with the texture of the final product. Here's a recipe you can try:

Gram's Chocolate Chirp Cookies

Lightly grease two cookie sheets. Preheat the oven to 375 degrees. Then, mix the following:

- 2 sticks of butter, softened
- 1 cup dark brown sugar
- 2 eggs
- 1 tsp. baking soda
- 2 tsp. vanilla extract
- 1 tsp. salt
- 3/4 cup sugar
- 1/2 cup cricket flour or powder

-Once it's thoroughly mixed, stir in 2 cups of all-purpose flour. (You might need a little more if the dough is still too sticky to handle.)
-Stir in 2 cups of semi-sweet chocolate chips.
-Drop large spoonfuls onto baking sheets and bake for 9-11 minutes, until edges are browned.
*For extra crickety cookies: If you'd like a little extra chirp in your cookies, add a few roasted crickets on top of the dough before baking!

DISCUSSION QUESTIONS

1. How does Mia's family feel about Gram's cricket farm? What evidence supports your thinking?

2. Why does Mia say she has a "stack of secret boxes"? What, do you think, is in those imagined boxes?

3. What are Mia's feelings about gymnastics? Cite evidence from the text to support your thinking.

4. While the girls are at the park, Mia watches Clover and decides she should try to be more like Clover. What are Clover's characteristics or traits that make Mia envious?

5. What makes cricket harvesting so time consuming? What is Mia's plan to improve the process?

6. What is important about Mia's family's traditions for the Fourth of July fireworks?

7. How were Anna's experiences with Eli, and Anna's mom's experiences at her tech company similar? What is/was problematic about the behavior they faced? How did Anna and her mom feel?

8. What does Mia mean when she says she felt the real truth poking at her insides?

9. Why is Mia so frustrated by the way people are treating Gram?

10. Describe how Phil's attention toward Mia might have crossed some boundaries. What are some hints that he made Mia uncomfortable?

11. Why do you think Mia told Anne Marie Spangler about her experience?

12. How is Mia's goal to improve on the rings at Warrior Camp a symbol of her healing?

13. What makes Mia and her friends suspicious of the moose, and how do they plan to use the moose to their advantage?

14. In what way(s) was the Vermont Launch Junior still a success for Mia even though her team did not place in the competition?

15. What was the outcome of Mia telling her mom about her experience at Tumblers?

16. How have Mia's parents' opinions of Gram's farm changed, and why?

17. Why was it important for Mia to mount the beam again? What did she find out by doing so?

18. The photograph of Mia jumping off the rocks into the lake is introduced in the first chapter and later recreated at the end of the book. What does Mia's jumping represent, and why is it important for her to reclaim that at the end of the book?

ENRICHMENT ACTIVITIES

Entomophagy

- Learn more about the process of farming crickets. What can you uncover about the nutritional value of eating crickets (and other insects)? How do crickets compare as a source of protein? Why is cricket farming environmentally conscious?
- Take the Chirp Challenge! Sample crickets—roasted or flavored—or find a recipe of your choosing and try edible insects, insect powders, or insect snacks. Three sites you might begin with: www.edibleinsects.com, www.cricketflours.com, and www.exoprotein.com.

Engineering and Innovation

- Design your own "Vermont Launch Junior" project. Develop a business plan, including ideas for marketing and persuading potential investors to support your project.
- Anna built a robot to help make cricket harvesting more efficient. Think about chores or responsibilities you know of. What would make these easier to accomplish or take less time? Construct with robotics kits and see what might be possible.
- Establish a makerspace in your home. Stock your makerspace with all kinds of materials for creating and inventing, and see what great ideas emerge.

Physical Activity

- Build a Warrior Camp-inspired challenge course. Draft blueprints for an imaginary course of your dreams, or get creative with equipment you have to build your own.
- Explore the sport of gymnastics. What kinds of movement, skills, or exercises are common in the sport? Why would maintaining focus be so critical to a gymnast?

Read on for a glimpse of Kate Messner's magical novel about a girl who catches a wish-granting fish!

Two sweaters, one puffy winter coat, two scarves, one pair of snow pants, one hat with ear flaps, and one pair of thick mittens later, I'm waddling across the yard to the McNeills' house. I feel like that snowsuit kid who couldn't move in the movie *A Christmas Story*, but it's too cold to be wearing anything less. The sun's out, though, so hopefully it'll warm up to zero soon.

Mrs. McNeill practically lives with Drew and his parents during fishing season. She and Drew are already out in his yard, getting fishing stuff ready. Drew tears open a package of Pop-Tarts and offers me one.

"What kind is it?" I ask.

"Strawberry. Duh."

"Thanks." When you've been friends as long as Drew and I have, you have a lot of conversations about which Pop-Tarts are the best (strawberry with frosting) and which are just gross (pumpkin, which has no business being anything but jack-o'-lanterns or pie).

"Hey, do you know what to do if you ever get buried in an avalanche?" Drew says through a mouth full of Pop-Tart.

"Nope," I say. Drew's nana gave him *The Worst-Case Scenario Handbook* a couple of years ago, and he's read it cover to cover, fifteen times. Sharing techniques for surviving unlikely catastrophes is his favorite thing in the world besides fishing. "What should I do?"

"Spit in the snow," Drew says, and spits on the snowy yard.

"How's that going to help?"

"You make a little air pocket and spit, and then gravity will tell you which way is up and which way is down. Then you aim up and dig like crazy."

"Good to know." I wonder if I'm in for a whole day of survival training. "Hey, is Rachael coming fishing with us?" Drew's older sister is a senior in high school and the coolest person I know other than Abby. Rachael's the one who got me into Irish dancing, only she's way better at it. She was seventeenth in North America last year.

"Nah," Drew says through a bite of Pop-Tart. "She's got some dumb *feece* to go to."

"It's *feis*." I pronounce it the right way—*fesh*—even though Drew already knows that's what the Irish dance competitions are called. The plural is *feiseanna* (fesh-ee-AH-nuh). Drew always calls them *feces* instead. It drives Rachael nuts. "Where is this one?"

"Rochester, I think."

Part of me wishes I could be there to watch, but then I remember that ice fishing is going to help me pay for the solo dress for my own feis in Montreal later this month.

"Got decent tread on those boots?" Mrs. McNeill asks me, and I hold up a foot to show her.

"Nope," she says, and hands me a pair of ice cleats. "Wrap these around the bottom of your boots or you'll be slipping all over the place."

I do that while she and Drew load poles, augers, and bait buckets onto the sled. Then we head out onto the lake. Right by shore, there's a hole in the ice with a pile of shavings around it. "Were you out already?" I ask.

Mrs. McNeill nods and kicks at the circle of snow. "Drilled a hole to check the thickness. We have a good six inches, so we're all set." She leads us away from shore onto the clearest black ice.

The ice flowers are still here, but they're flat and muffled today, like wildflowers someone pressed in a book. They crunch under my feet as we head toward a point of land sticking out from shore.

I'm taking careful steps, one foot in front of the other, and managing to convince myself this is safe. But when we're halfway out to the point, the ice lets out a booming-loud, timpani-drum thump. I've heard muted ice sounds from shore before, but this is *loud*. I jump about a mile and look at Mrs. McNeill. "Is it breaking up?"

"I know how to survive being stranded on an iceberg," Drew says.

"I'm *so* hoping we don't need that information right now," I tell him.

Mrs. McNeill gives me a reassuring smile and shakes her head. "The ice is fine, my dear. You're simply hearing air bubbles working themselves up through the fissures now that the sun's up. Listen . . ." She pauses, and the ice booms again, like thunder out by the island a mile offshore. Then it makes a weird, video-game sound. *Gurgle-twang-zzzing!* "That's the ice talking, letting us know it's settling in for a good, long winter of fishing."

I keep going. But my heart's still pumping fast, and my legs feel wobbly, even with the cleats. If this ice really means to be reassuring, it ought to talk in something other than loud, scary growls and space invader weapon sounds. Right now, I'm hearing less "We're going to have a good winter" and more "I'm going to swallow you whole."

Not far from the point, Mrs. McNeill pulls the sled to a stop and looks around. "You think this is about where we were in the boat?" she asks Drew.

"Pretty close." Drew turns to me. "There's a ledge around here where the perch like to feed. We were pulling 'em in like crazy back in August."

They start unloading gear from the sled. I pick up an insulated bucket and can feel the bait sloshing around inside. "Are these minnows?"

"Yep. They're always better than lures when you can get 'em." Mrs. McNeill pulls a power auger from the sled and turns to Drew. "Shall we let Charlie give this a try?"

"Sure, as long as I get to drill my own," he says.

"I don't know how to use that," I say. The auger has a pull cord like the outboard motor on the McNeills' boat, and I couldn't pull hard enough to get that started last summer.

But Mrs. McNeill leans over to show me. "Piece of cake," she says. "Pull the rip cord." I do that, and the motor starts humming. "Great!" She points to a trigger thing on the auger's handle. "Now give it some gas to make the blades turn, and we're in business." She guides the auger to a spot on the ice and holds it with me, pressing down while the blades whirl into the ice. In a few seconds, there's a hole about six inches wide and a sparkling circle of ice shavings all around it. "Perfect!"

She hands the auger to Drew, who makes his own hole about ten feet farther out. Then he pulls three short fishing poles from the sled and hands one to me. It's only a couple feet long, way smaller than the poles we use in summer.

I take off my mittens, fish out a minnow, and bait the hook. My bare hands burn with the cold. Once they're mittened up again, Mrs. McNeill gives me a quick ice fishing lesson.

"You want to drop your bait maybe two or three feet down," she says, "and be sure to give the pole a good tug when you feel a bite. They can get away quick." She puts the lid on the bait bucket and slides it over so I can use it as a stool. "One more thing before you fish . . ." She reaches under her scarf, pulls out a four-leaf clover charm on a chain, and holds it up. "May the luck of the ice spirits be with you."

"That doesn't sound like science," I say.

She smiles and tucks the charm back under her layers of wool. "Drew's grandfather gave it to me when we got engaged years and years ago. He said it was a good luck charm, and I decided I'd believe that. It hasn't always worked for me, but I've learned that you take your magic where you can get it. Especially when you're waiting on fish to bite." She heads farther out on the ice, a little past Drew, to drill another hole, and I drop my line down under the ice to wait.

There's a lot of waiting in ice fishing, and now that I'm not moving, it feels colder, even with the sunshine. The air is still biting, and my fingers never warmed up inside my mittens. I hold my pole with one hand and lift the other to my mouth to blow some heat onto them. Twenty minutes go by in silence, except for the ice groaning and thumping.

Finally, Mrs. McNeill stands up. "Got one!" she hollers, and reels in a perch.

Drew stands up to see. "Ain't big enough to bother with in the derby, but Billy'll take it."

"*Isn't*," Mrs. McNeill says. Drew totally knows better, but he loves the cowboys in old Western movies and knows it drives his nana crazy when he talks like them.

Mrs. McNeill pops the lid off her bucket, drops the fish inside, covers it, and sits down. Almost right away, she has another fish, and then Drew stands up. "I got one too!"

I keep waiting for a tug on my line. Drew pulls in three more fish, and Mrs. McNeill catches a bigger one. "This fella's got a chance, don't you think?" She holds it up, and Drew nods. She puts it in the bucket and calls to me. "Charlie, I bet you're in too shallow. Why don't you come out where it's a little deeper, and we'll set you up with a new hole?"

I shake my head. "I like this hole." That's because I'm pretty sure the water underneath it isn't over my head.

Another half hour goes by. Drew and Mrs. McNeill have at least twenty fish between them. I haven't even had a bite yet, but the thought of going out any farther on this ice makes my knees wobble. My hands are freezing, and my nose is running, and I can't remember why this seemed like a good idea. There's not much use fishing when you're afraid to go where the fish are.

Apparently, ice flowers don't have enough magic to turn me into a fisherman.

Fisherwoman.

Whatever. It's not going to happen.

"Woo-hoo!" Drew starts reeling in another one, and I'm about to give up when I feel the tiniest pull.

"Oh!" I stand up and give a tug, and at first I think the fish got away because it feels like I'm reeling in a whole lot of nothing. But when the line comes up, there's a tiny perch flopping on the end. It's not much bigger than the minnow I used as bait, but at least it's something.

"She's got one!" Mrs. McNeill shouts from across the ice.

Drew turns and looks. "You call that a fish?" He snorts out a laugh.

I ease my miniscule catch off the hook. "Should I let it go?"

"Nah, Billy'll take it. Put it in the . . . whoa!" Drew's pole almost jumps out of his hand. He turns around and starts reeling again. Mrs. McNeill's got another bite too. I stand up, holding the fish in one hand, and pull the lid off the bucket with the other.

"Please," someone says.

And I freeze. Because it's not Mrs. McNeill and it's not Drew. And it's not the stupid growly ice talking this time either. This voice is quiet and low-pitched and raspy.

"Please," it says again.

I look at the fish in my hand. It's a skinny thing, only about five inches long, black-and-green striped with orange on its fins. But instead of plain, glassy-black eyes like the other perch I've seen, this fish has bright-green eyes that almost glow. Like emeralds. Crystals. And this fish is looking right at me.

"Release me," the raspy voice says, and I swear I see the fish's mouth moving a tiny bit, as if it's gasping for breath.

But it can't be. Fish breathe through gills. That was one of Mrs. McNeill's lakeside science lectures last summer. And the bigger issue here is not how a fish breathes but that this one is talking. To me.

"Release me," the raspy voice says again, "and I will grant you a wish."

KATE MESSNER is passionately curious and writes books that encourage kids to wonder, too. Her titles include award-winning picture books like *Over and Under the Snow*, *The Next President*, and *How to Read a Story*; novels like *The Seventh Wish*, *Breakout*, and *Chirp*; the Fergus and Zeke easy reader series; the Ranger in Time historical adventures; and several works of nonfiction, including *Insect Superpowers*, *Tracking Pythons*, and the History Smashers series. Before becoming a full-time writer, Kate was a TV journalist and National Board certified middle school English teacher. She lives on Lake Champlain with her family and is trying to summit all forty-six Adirondack High Peaks in between book deadlines.

www.katemessner.com

@KateMessner

From high-stakes **adventure**
to unexpected **magic**
to sweet **friendships**—
there's a lot to love
from Kate Messner!

www.bloomsbury.com
Twitter: BloomsburyKids
Instagram: BloomsburyPublishing